A CONVENIENT ACCIDENT

When they took Hal's body to town, the sheriff and undertaker made the same assessment. A single blow to the back of the head had done it. The coroner thought a heavy object might have been used, but he could not rule out the possibility that Hal had fallen from his horse.

"That horse didn't buck," Dane insisted.

"Maybe not," said the coroner. "I wasn't there."

"Neither was I," said Dane. "And the horse can't talk."

The next evening, Laurel, Dane, and Atkins sat down to another gloomy meal together. Dane gave a summary of the sheriff's investigation, which entailed riding out to circle the scene, kneeling on the ground where the body was found, and making a few notations in a pocket notebook.

"So what does he think?" asked Laurel. Her face was drawn and pale, but she was finding something to hang on to.

Dane shrugged. "He thinks about the same as the coroner does. It could have been an accident, or it could have been something else."

Something else. Atkins poked at his potatoes. It was easy enough to imagine a two-man job, one holding a gun and the other aiming the blow. "Well, it was one way or the other," he said.

"Yes, it was," Dane said. "And I don't think it was an accident."

JOHN D. NESBITT

FOR THE NORDEN BOYS

LEISURE BOOKS   NEW YORK CITY

For my good friends
Bill and Angie Babcock.

A LEISURE BOOK®

June 2002

Published by

Dorchester Publishing Co., Inc.
276 Fifth Avenue
New York, NY 10001

ISBN 0-8439-5025-0

Visit us on the web at www.dorchesterpub.com.

FOR THE NORDEN BOYS

Chapter One

Atkins threw in his lot with the Norden boys one fall afternoon in 1888. They came riding toward his camp, where he sat on his bedroll and peered beyond his tripod and the pot of coffee hanging there. He got up and watched the men ride in. He thought he recognized them, but he wasn't sure. Riders from quite a few outfits had come and gone during the roundup season, and if these two had come to his chuck wagon, it hadn't been for long.

They rode in at a slow walk for the last hundred yards, raising little dust on the quiet plain. Behind them, to the west, Silver Mountain was beginning to darken in its afternoon shadow. The sun still hung above the peaks, but the shadows grew fast at this time of day. The two riders, with the sun at their back, carried a bit of shade as well; as they rode closer, he thought he recognized them as the Norden brothers.

Atkins could hear the muffled thud of horse hooves as the riders called out a greeting. He answered back, telling them to come on in and have a cup of coffee. The two young men swung down and walked forward, leading their horses.

"You're Tom Atkins, aren't you?" It was the huskier of the two, probably the older, who spoke. He had dark blond hair and blue eyes; he needed a shave, but he was not a bad-looking fellow. He was in his early to mid-twenties, maybe a couple of years older than his brother.

"Sure am." Atkins stepped around the fire pit.

"I'm Dane Norden. This is my brother, Hal."

"Pleased to meet you." Atkins shook hands with each of them. "I think we've met before. You came to the wagon a while back, didn't you?"

Dane answered. "Yeah, we did. A little over a month ago. We were ridin' for Fred Morris."

Atkins nodded. "That's right. I remember now. A little outfit, over to the south."

"Well, it's ours now."

Atkins raised his eyebrows. "Oh, really?"

"Uh-huh." Dane motioned with his head. "Hal and I bought what was left. Morris shipped everything he could. We got the land claim, the buildings, a couple of hundred head of cattle, and a small herd of horses.''

Atkins looked from Dane to Hal and back to Dane. "I hope you do well."

"Thanks," Dane answered.

Silence hung in the air for a second. "Well, let's have coffee," said Atkins. He dug three tin cups out of his camp kit and poured from the blackened coffeepot. The cheery smell of coffee rose in the air.

The boys sat on the ground, each holding the reins of his horse, while Atkins went back to his bedroll. He set it at a right angle from the boys, so he would not have to look through the tripod to talk to them. Then he sat down and tasted the coffee, which was bitter but satisfying.

Dane sipped on his coffee, gave a wince, and relaxed his face. "I understand the Dupré outfit went broke."

Atkins tightened his mouth, then relaxed. "Well, I don't know if he went plumb broke, but he sold out. To the Argentine Ranch." Atkins tipped his chin in the direction of Silver Mountain, and as he did so he pictured what he had just mentioned. At the base of the mountain, where a stream flowed down through a broad canyon, Frank Cobarde had his headquarters. It was no secret that he was expanding his Argentine Ranch and didn't mind pinching out a few others if he had to.

3

"Well, I guess that's how I heard it," Dane answered, with what seemed like an amending tone. He raised his cup to take a drink of coffee.

"Uh-huh." Atkins looked at Hal, who smiled but said nothing.

"Anyway," Dane resumed, "I understand that you might be lookin' for work."

Atkins glanced at his cup and then at the two boys. "It did leave me out of a job, but I hadn't really started lookin' for another one yet."

"No hurry," said Dane, "but we thought we'd talk to you before you left the country."

Atkins looked around at his camp, most of which was still wrapped up in canvas packs, and at his two horses, which were picketed out on the grass to the east. "I'm not goin' anywhere very fast, it doesn't seem. So go ahead."

Dane looked at his brother and back at Atkins. "We're lookin' for someone to be a cook and a general hand."

Atkins frowned. He wondered if these boys wanted someone to do two jobs in one. He drank from his coffee and looked at Dane. "I can sure enough cook," he said. "I'm not too old to rope, but there are other things I do better."

"Oh, no," came the answer as Dane raised his left palm. "I just mean for someone to help around the place. You know, help fix up the buildings, straighten things out. Fred let things run down quite a bit."

4

"I didn't mean I was afraid to work."

"Oh, no. Neither did I. But I didn't want you to think we were goin' to have you do everything while we sat around and played cards."

Atkins laughed. "I didn't think you were Englishmen." He looked at Hal, who lowered his tin cup and gave a look of good humor. Atkins returned the smile. "Of course, I've cooked for them, too." He looked back at Dane. "I suppose sooner or later we'd have to talk about wages."

Dane nodded toward his brother. "We can offer you twenty-five a month during the winter."

. Atkins paused. Just about any cowpuncher was worth a dollar a day during the season, and a cook was worth all of that, especially with other work thrown in. But winter days were short for outside work, and he didn't know if he would even find a job until spring. "And after that?"

Dane pursed his lips and gave a brisk nod. "It'll go up five."

Atkins thought for a moment. That wasn't top pay for summer wages, either. But it would be worth it, over the space of a year or so, if he didn't get laid off at this time next year. He looked at the two boys, and he liked the sense of harmony he felt between them. "I could give it a try," he said.

Dane smiled. "Good. That's what we were hopin'. You know where our place is, don't you?"

Atkins looked off to the south, where a line of hills ran from west to east across the plain. The last hill on the left stood apart from the others. "You go through that gap, don't you? And then your place is on the other side?"

"That's right." Dane tipped up his cup.

Atkins looked at Hal. "And how about you? You haven't said much so far."

Hal had a boyish look about him. "Not much to say. I think Dane pretty well covered it." Hal looked at his brother and then back at Atkins. "If you want to, you could ride on out with us now."

Atkins shrugged. "I guess I could. Beats sleepin' on the ground, though I don't mind that, either." He looked at each of the boys, who nodded, and then he went on. "No hurry, though, like you say. We might as well drink this coffee as throw it out." As he poured a second cup all the way around, he realized he felt good to be back on the job and in charge of a campfire again.

The coffee was not very hot and went down fast. When it was finished, Hal went to bring in the two horses and pickets. Dane held the two saddle horses while Atkins started to pack up the camp. He had set aside the tripod and coffeepot before he sat down to drink the second cup of coffee, so those items were cool enough to be packed as well.

6

Dane held all four horses as Hal helped Atkins load the camp onto the packhorse. Then Atkins saddled his riding horse and was ready to go. He looked around at the campsite, which was just another spot on the plains once again. Atkins walked his horse out a ways and back, checked the cinch, and mounted up. Hal handed him the lead rope of the packhorse, and the brothers swung into their saddles.

The sun was just slipping behind the peaks when the three riders and four horses moved out of the campsite. Atkins looked over his shoulder and saw Silver Mountain, looming darker now in its own shadow. Then he looked ahead at the line of hills to the south as his horse fell into pace with those of the Norden boys.

Atkins awoke in the gray light of morning. He could hear the even breathing of the two young men. It had been dark when they arrived at the ranch the evening before, and he hadn't seen much except the inside of the bunkhouse. All of his gear, and the boys' saddles as well, lay in heaps inside the door. Somewhere outside, he understood, was a corral where Hal had turned out the horses. Beyond that, he didn't have much of an idea of how the place was laid out.

He slipped the blankets aside, then rolled over and up into a sitting position. He made little noise as he pulled on his shirt and trousers and settled into his boots. Soft-stepping across the room, he picked his hat and coat off the wall pegs, pulled the hat onto his head, hunched into the coat, and stepped outside.

A cool, dry breeze met him as he closed the door behind him. He could smell dust and sage and dry grass. Fall was in the air, sure enough. When the cold weather set in, he would be glad he had a bunkhouse and cookstove, and even now, with the whiff of autumn, something inside him said it was good to be settling in.

He looked around the ranch yard and saw nothing unusual. Straight across, to the south, sat a stable with corrals reaching out behind on either side. To the west, at right angles to the bunkhouse and stable, sat a small house, with weeds growing all around it. The three buildings all had their doors facing the rectangular ranch yard, which was marked off on the east end by a trash heap of cans and bottles and who knew what else. Atkins looked back to his right. The trail they had ridden in on from the northwest came into the yard between the bunkhouse and the vacant house, while another trail led out to the southwest between the house and the stable.

All of the buildings showed wear from the weather, and the place had a run-down look to it. Old posts and planks lay here and there in front of the buildings, as if someone had had the energy to toss them there but not the energy to

set them in a stack or put them to some purpose.
A woodpile of stumps and branches lay in front
of the stable, straight across from the bunkhouse. At the east end of the stable, not far from
the midden of cans and bottles, stood a crippled
ranch wagon. Its left rear wheel was missing, and
the axle on that side was blocked up about a foot
off the ground. The bed of the wagon sloped
down to that corner, giving a view of a heap of
rocks. Atkins wondered if the rocks had caused
the wheel to give out, and he wondered how
much trouble it might have been to toss out the
rocks and block up the axle so it would sit level.

He tried not to let other people's messes
bother him, although he had seen things he
didn't care for—cowpunchers who mended their
saddles with wire, and wagon bosses who fixed
everything from axles to wagon tongues with
rawhide. He had seen more than one young rider
leave a horse tied up with the reins wound
around the saddle horn and one rein drooping
lower than the other, and he had seen men who
would not take the trouble to stack the bedrolls
before the wagon pulled out. Atkins always kept
his own wagon neat, and if someone else didn't,
he tried not to say anything even if he couldn't
ignore it.

He walked out a ways on the trail he had come
in on the night before. He could see the south
side of the hills they had ridden through, and

closer in, he saw lower hills with a few scattered trees. Turning around, he could see low hills on the north and west of the ranch site, while the plains opened up to the south and east. For as much as the ranch seemed to have suffered neglect, someone had taken the trouble to situate it in a good place and to put up the buildings in a sensible layout.

Walking back into the ranch yard, he noticed that not a single tree grew in the vicinity of the buildings. He wondered if anybody had ever planted any, as the place seemed to have been established with more care than it had been kept up. The boys had said, the evening before, that Morris had run the place for seven or eight years and they weren't sure who had it before that. Atkins figured it didn't matter. His job was to help the boys try·to make something of it again.

The bunkhouse door opened, and Hal stepped outside. "Good mornin'," he said.

"Good mornin'. I thought I'd take a look around, to see where I was."

Hal smiled. He wasn't wearing a hat, and his light brown hair was tousled. "Well, this is it. Like Dane says, it might not look like much, but it's a ranch, and it's ours."

The young man's optimism made Atkins feel good. "You bet it is, Hal." He glanced at the bunkhouse. "Is your brother up?"

"He's gettin' up. I imagine he'll be out in a minute."

"Well, I suppose I'd better go in and get breakfast goin'."

The kitchen lay at the west end of the bunkhouse, with the eating area between the kitchen and the sleeping quarters. Atkins got a fire going in the cookstove, then rummaged around for the utensils and food to put a breakfast together. Before long, the smell of coffee and fried food wafted on the air.

The boys sat down facing each other at the table and dug into the bacon, fried potatoes, and biscuits. Atkins poured himself some coffee, set the pot on the table between the boys, and sat down at the end of the table closest to the kitchen.

Dane had his sleeves rolled up. He kept his left hand on the table near his coffee cup as he worked the fork with his right hand. Between bites he said, "Hal says you got out to take a look at things."

"Uh-huh."

"Needs a little work, doesn't it?"

Atkins smiled. "Nothin' to be scared of."

Both boys looked up and nodded. With their hats off, there was a noticeable difference between Dane's dark blond hair and Hal's light brown, but their blue eyes were very much alike.

After breakfast, Atkins washed the dishes

11

while the boys drank another cup of coffee. Neither of them lit up a smoke, nor had they the evening before, so Atkins assumed that neither of them carried the habit.

When Atkins had the kitchen in order, the boys got up from the table, and the three of them put on hats and coats. Dane led the way to the stable, which had stalls on the right end and an enclosed shed on the left. An open doorway led to the stalls, as Atkins had seen earlier, while the shed had a hinged door that was closed and fastened. Dane went to the door, pulled a Y-shaped stick out of the hasp, and swung the door outward.

"Well, here's where we keep the tools," he said.

Daylight lit up the interior as Atkins stepped inside. To the left sat an old upright stump with a vise bolted to it. Lying on a workbench were a hammer, tongs, and other horseshoeing items such as a rasp, a hoof knife, and a pair of nippers. On the wall above the workbench, arrayed in neat order, hung a saw, a brace and bit, a hammer, and a carpenter's square.

Turning to the back wall, Atkins saw more tools he knew how to use. A shovel leaned against the wall, and a pitchfork with gleaming steel tines hung head-up on a pair of nails. He noted a double-bit ax, also hanging in place, and beneath it a crowbar. Off to the right, in lesser light, sat a mattock with its head on the ground and its handle touching the wall. Atkins picked it up. It was heavy like a pickax, but it had only one blade, like a southern field hoe. It got its weight from the thick blade and the heavy iron shank that formed a sleeve for the handle.

"Most of these tools came with the place," Hal said.

Atkins hefted the mattock. "This would be all right for digging a fire pit." He nodded, then set the tool back in its place.

Dane's voice came from the left. "This is new, though."

Atkins turned and saw Dane holding out a branding iron. Atkins took it in his hands and turned it until he made out the monogram NB. "Norden Brothers," he said, looking at Dane and then Hal.

"We thought it would be a good name," said Hal.

Atkins nodded. "I'd say so." He handed the iron back to Dane, who hung it on a nail on the east wall.

Hal spoke again. "That door leads into the stable, but it's nailed shut. It had leather hinges that gave out, it looks like. We've got to put metal hinges on." He smiled. "Just one of a hundred little things."

Dane led the way back outside, followed by Atkins and then Hal. They walked around to the open doorway and into the other half of the building, which consisted of four empty stalls. Some of the planks were hanging loose, and two of the gates had been separated from their leather hinges. Across from the stalls, against the wall that separated the toolroom from this half of the building, leaned a heavy-looking door, about four feet wide and six feet long.

"Another little job," said Dane, looking at the door and then the doorway. "At least it's got metal hinges. It just needs heavier screws."

They walked outside again and stood in the sunlight. The morning had begun to warm a little.

Atkins looked at the little house with the weeds growing around it. "And the house?"

Dane looked at Hal and then at the hired man. "We'll get to it, too." He looked at the bunkhouse. "But I think the first thing we should do is get you and your stuff settled in, and see what supplies we need to keep us goin' for a couple of weeks. Then Hal and I can go to town and pick up what we need."

Atkins looked at the wagon he had noticed earlier in the morning. "I don't suppose you'll be goin' in that thing right away."

Hal laughed. "I guess not. No idea where that wheel went. But we'll ask around and see about finding another one."

"It would be handy," said Atkins. "For firewood and the like, not to mention trips to town."

Dane nodded. "We were just talking yesterday about how we were going to fix it, and how much trouble it would be to haul a wheel out here."

Atkins smiled. "Of course, if the wagon was running, you could haul the wheel back in it, only then you wouldn't need the wheel."

The boys laughed. "That's about the way things seem," Dane said. "It's hard to know where to start."

Atkins went back into the bunkhouse, where he put his personal things under his bunk and then got his cooking utensils settled in the kitchen. He built up a fire again and fixed a midday dinner that was just like the breakfast. While the potatoes were frying and the biscuits were baking, he made out a list of supplies to be fetched from town. As he worked, he could hear the Norden brothers banging planks in the stable so that the stalls would be serviceable.

After dinner the boys said they were ready to saddle up and go to town. Atkins had just finished wiping down the kitchen when he heard them ride past the bunkhouse. He went to the doorway and watched them head east out of the ranch. They were good boys, he thought.

He looked across the yard at the leaning wagon. Before he did anything else, he was going to toss those rocks out and take some of the weight off of that wagon box.

15

It took Atkins all of ten minutes to pitch the rocks over the tail end of the wagon. After that he went into the toolshed and brought out the ax. He figured he might as well go to work on the woodpile, as he needed to cut up at least a day's worth of stove lengths.

It was a pleasant afternoon, not warm and not cold, as he worked in the ranch yard. He imagined the boys were having an enjoyable ride to town. They seemed like a good enough pair. They got along well together, and they treated their cook like a white man. Atkins's thoughts flickered off to the northwest for a moment. He hoped the boys did all right, but it might be a rough time for a couple of lads trying to build up a small ranch, when there was a big outfit looming not so far away and hoping to get bigger.

Chapter Two

Atkins held his side of the door steady, lifting up with a crowbar, as Dane drove the screws into the dry lumber of the door frame. Dane had strong forearms, which helped him put force into the screwdriver. One by one he tightened the screws, then got down from the box he had been standing on.

"Let 'er swing, and we'll see how she works."

Atkins stepped back with the crowbar, and Hal pushed the door. It squeaked as it swung outward from the stable. Dane caught it with the heel of his right hand and sent it back to his brother, who stopped it and then stepped out of the shadow.

"Looks good enough," said Dane. "That's one little chore done."

"Were you able to find any hinges?" Atkins asked.

Dane shook his head. "I was lucky to get screws. This fellow Chapman acts like it's the hardest thing in the world to order hardware. He said he couldn't get hinges for me until spring. I wonder if he just didn't feel like takin' the trouble. Didn't it seem that way to you, Hal?"

"He seemed pretty casual."

Dane sniffed. "That's what happens when there's no competition. A fellow can do just about as he pleases." He looked around the yard. "There's plenty of other work to be done, though."

Atkins followed his gaze around the yard and then stopped to look at the trail that came in from the northwest. A lone rider, about three quarters of a mile out, was headed toward the ranch. "Looks like someone might be comin' this way," Atkins said.

Dane looked at his brother. "Do you know him, Hal?"

"Hard to tell at this distance, but I don't think so."

"Well, I guess we'll see what he's got on his mind, if he's comin' to talk to us." Dane turned his back on the rider and looked at the job they had just finished. "I guess we can pick up our tools and wait for this fellow to ride in."

Atkins hefted the crowbar he had used to hold

18

up the corner of the door. "Say, Dane," he said. "If you give me that hammer, I can be pulling a few nails out of some of these planks while you and Hal talk to your visitor."

Dane looked in the direction of the rider, then picked up the hammer and lobbed it to Atkins, who caught it. The boys picked up the other things, including the box and a can of nails, and put them in the toolroom.

Atkins used the crook end of the crowbar to turn over a plank that lay next to the stable. Nothing remarkable crawled out, so he bent over and picked up the plank. He pounded a couple of nails that were sticking through on each end, then turned the plank over, put it on the ground, and pulled the nails out with the crowbar. Glancing up, he saw that the rider had come closer but had not reached the buildings yet, so he found another plank and went to work on it.

When the rider came into the yard, Atkins finished the plank he was working on and stood by the stable door, which hung ajar. Hal and Dane stood a few yards out. The rider came on in but did not dismount.

"How do you do?" said Dane.

"Mornin'," said the rider. "Is this the Nordens?"

Dane did the talking, as usual. "Sure is. I'm Dane, and this is my brother, Hal."

The rider nodded. "My name's Fey. Orvus Fey."

"Pleased to meet you. This is our hired man, Tom Atkins."

Fey glanced at the hired man, gave half a nod, and looked back at Dane before Atkins could say hello. Something in the way the man carried himself was disagreeable. Atkins didn't know if it was the flicker in his eye, the snubbing of a hired hand, or the way he looked down at the Norden boys, but it wasn't the open manner of a man hoping to make new friends. Atkins noticed that Fey wore silver spurs and had the tip of a holster sticking out beneath his gray wool coat. He wore a dark, charcoal-colored hat with a broad, flat brim and a flat crown. Drab brown hair stuck straight down over his ears and touched his collar, and a sparse, bristly mustache sprouted on his upper lip. The man had a lean look to him, from his narrow face on down to his boots, where his trousers were tucked in tight.

Dane spoke again. "Well, what can we do for you?"

At that moment a little breeze came up and opened the stable door with a creak. Atkins caught it, and as he did so he saw Fey give a quick look and then turn back toward Dane.

"Well, I'm new here, and I thought I should git out to meet the neighbors." The horse shifted so that Fey had his right side toward Atkins.

Dane nodded. "Nice of you to do that. Have you taken up land around here?"

"Not yit." Fey smiled, showing a set of large teeth. "But I might."

"Oh," Dane answered, allowing the single syllable to trail off and invite explanation.

"I come to work for the Argentine Ranch." As Fey spoke, his right hand brushed the skirt of his coat and then settled again on the saddle horn.

"I see."

"So it seemed like a good idea to go out and meet people."

"Well, that's a good thing to do. Now that you know us, this is our place. We just took it over, and we'll be fixin' it up."

Fey looked around and nodded but did not answer.

Dane spoke again. "I hope your first winter here isn't too harsh."

Fey showed his teeth again. "I'm from Missoura, and a bucket of water'll freeze in the kitchen there, too. So I think I'll find things tolerable." Fey raised his chin and lifted his mustache in a smile.

The breeze came up again at that moment, and the dark hat sailed to the ground at Atkins's feet. Atkins pushed the stable door closed, picked up the hat, and stepped forward to hand it up to its owner.

Fey leaned forward on the right side of the

21

horse and reached for the hat, and for the first time he gave Atkins a direct look. Atkins took note of the lean face, the broad hook nose, the straight drab hair that had been mashed down by the errant hat. Fey's eyes were brown, and they seemed to have puffy lower eyelids, although his leaning forward might have given that effect. Atkins had noticed that people sometimes looked grotesque when they leaned over to look at someone, and he thought Fey looked that way as he reached for his hat.

"Thanks," he said, regaining his composure as he settled the hat back onto his head.

"Welcome," said Atkins, stepping back.

"That's one thing to get used to in Wyoming." Dane's voice had a cheerful note. "The wind. You never know when it's going to come up or which way it'll blow."

The breeze had died down, but Fey had his head cocked in that direction anyway. He lifted his chin again. "Well, I think I'll move along and meet a few more neighbors."

"Good enough," said Dane. "I'm glad you stopped in. Hope you enjoy your stay here."

"I'm sure I will." Fey showed his teeth again as he nodded at the Norden brothers, and then without looking again at Atkins, he rode out of the ranch yard to the east.

When the rider was well beyond the trash

heap, Dane turned to the other two and said, "Nice fellow. All smiles."

"A different kind of cowpuncher," said Atkins. "I noticed he doesn't carry a rope."

Dane wrinkled his nose. "Well, we've got no quarrel with them, and we can just keep our distance." He looked around. "What were we going to do next?"

"Finish work on the stalls," Hal answered.

"That's right. We need to get them workin'."

Atkins glanced at the wagon. "Did you happen to find out about a wheel?"

Dane looked at Hal. "Yes, we did. Hal has a trip to make on Sunday, and he'll bring it out then." Dane smiled, and his brother did, too.

They had the stalls in working order by dinnertime. Atkins warmed up half a pot of beans left over from the mess he had cooked the afternoon before, and he served the beans along with a plate of cold biscuits. When the men had finished the main business of eating, they poured another cup of coffee.

Dane, who had brought home tobacco and papers from town the day before, went about rolling a smoke. Having watched him roll cigarettes the night before and again in the morning, Atkins assumed he was pretty well practiced and had just been out of makin's for a couple of days. Dane had strong-looking hands, and with his sleeves rolled up, he looked as if he put a lot of muscle into building a smoke. He did a quick, neat job of it, though, and lit the cigarette without any flourish.

As the conversation resumed, the men talked about what job they would do next.

"We've got quite a bit of work to do on the little house," Dane said. He smiled in his teasing way. "We don't want Hal to have to put off anything."

"Oh?" Atkins looked at Hal and saw that he was blushing.

"Hal's going to need the little house," Dane said. "He's got a honey, and they want to be together."

Atkins set down his cup. "Really?"

Hal nodded.

"Well, this is the first I've heard of it. What's her name? What's she like?"

Hal smiled in his boyish way. "Her name's Laurel, and she's the sweetest girl in the world."

Atkins arched his eyebrows. "Well, she'd better be—or, you'd better think so."

Hal's smile closed in a little, and his head swayed. "You'll see. I'm gonna bring her out here on Sunday."

Atkins flinched. "So soon?"

"No, not to live here. Just to see the place. She hasn't seen it yet, and we wanted her to take a look at the house and tell us what she wanted to have done."

Atkins looked at Dane. "Give it the woman's touch."

Dane grinned. "I don't think she can count on any of us sewing curtains, but we can put up a few shelves and whatnot."

Atkins thought for a second. "So you're going to hire a wagon and bring her out?"

"That's my plan."

"Well, it's about time we got to the bottom of this mystery. I was wondering how you were going to fetch that wagon wheel."

Hal gave a broad smile now. "Two birds with one stone," he said.

Atkins finished his coffee and got up from the table. He had put a dishpan of water on the stove, so he was ready for the after-dinner cleanup. Dane sat at the table entering expenses in a ledger, while Hal helped Atkins with the dishes.

"Things won't change all that much," Hal said.

"How do you mean?"

"Well, with what you'll be doing. Dane and I don't want Laurel to have to cook for a bunch of men. And we'll have more in the spring, of course."

Atkins nodded. "And she wouldn't go out on the range with the wagon anyway."

"Oh, no. And even during roundup, I won't leave her here by herself. I'll come back in the evenings when we're close, and she can go to town when that doesn't work."

"Oh, do her folks live there?"

"Her sister does. Their folks are gone, and she lives with her sister."

"Oh. Uh-huh." Atkins wondered what the sister, or the sister's husband, did for a living, but he didn't like to be inquisitive. Then he thought of a polite way to ask. "Is she a country girl?"

"Sort of. She grew up in a small town in Illinois, and she's been around cows and chickens. So she knows something about animals. Right now, she's just helping her sister around the house."

"Oh."

"Yeah, her sister is married to a man who's got a business there in town."

"Not the fellow you tried to buy the hinges from?"

Hal laughed. "No, he's got the barbershop."

"Oh, I know him. Sort of a heavyset fellow. I've had a bath there a few times."

"Right. His name's Ralph McCoy. Everyone calls him by his first name."

"Sure. I can't say I know his wife, though, or your girl either."

"Well, you'll meet her on Sunday."

Atkins and the boys spent the afternoon cleaning out the little house. The whole job was a dusty, musty business. Fred Morris had not left anything of value, but he had not bothered to clear out the empty cans, the newspapers, and the old catalogues. More than one person had lived in the house for the past few years, as was evident from the flimsy shelves that were tacked to the wall where bunks had stood. Each of the two sleeping rooms had a pile of rags, mostly worn-out socks and tattered shirts, with the lower parts of ruined boots tossed in for good measure. The shanks of the boots, Atkins imagined, had been cut off to be converted into hinges and patches.

Atkins found himself wishing he had a wheelbarrow. In its absence, he used a canvas sheet from his pack outfit and carried the trash a bundle at a time to the rubbish heap, where Dane tended the fire with pitchfork in hand. Hal tore down the makeshift shelves, pulled some nails from the walls and drove others in, swept down cobwebs, and swept up dead flies and moths. By the end of the day, they had the little house cleaned out and ready for repairs.

That evening, Atkins fried some bacon to go along with the last of the beans. The smell of fried pork was welcome after a few hours of breathing in dust and the dry odors of rubbish. Still, Atkins thought the boys might be getting tired of bacon. As he sat down to eat, he said, "I don't know how soon we might want to hang some beef."

Dane looked up. "Anytime, really. We won't go through an animal very fast, just the three of us, but the weather's cool enough that it should last a while." He looked at his brother. "We could probably go out and find a long yearling."

Hal nodded. "I could take some to Ralph and Susie, too."

"Uh-huh." Dane went back to his meal.

Atkins looked at both boys and thought about what hadn't been said. When folks were off on their own, they often took care not to butcher their own beef. Rather, they kept an eye out for a brand they didn't know or that came from a long ways off. There was a general understanding that it all came out even, as long as an outfit wasn't killing everyone else's beef and selling it. Some fellows did that, too, but it wasn't a good way to start a new ranch and make friends with the neighbors.

Recalling the door they had put up earlier in the day, Atkins said, "We could hang the meat there in the stable, don't you think, now that it's closed in?"

Dane looked up and smiled, then said to Hal, "Old Dad thinks of everything, doesn't he?"

Hal smiled and nodded. "Seems like."

Atkins laid down his spoon and felt himself smile. "Since when did we start calling me 'Old Dad'?"

Dane shrugged. "Just now, I guess."

Atkins cocked his head. "Well, I don't know if it fits."

Dane had a droll look on his face. "Why's that?"

"Well, I might be old enough to be someone's dad, but not yours. I'll be thirty-eight on my next birthday, after the turn of the year." Atkins realized it was old for a ranch hand and probably seemed old to these boys, but he was only half a generation older than they were—fifteen years at the most.

"I just meant it as a nickname."

"Oh, I know. But a cook named Dad is always an older man, with a sagging gut and a slow walk. I've seen 'em, and you have, too. Some toothless old codger with his chin touching his nose. He can barely hold a cigarette in his lips." Atkins laughed. "I'd just as soon not be called Dad as long as I've got teeth in my mouth and hair on my head."

The boys looked at him. He could tell they were seeing the iron-gray streaks on his temples, but he was proud of his full head of hair.

"That's all right," Dane said. "It's good to have someone a little older around the place. They see things clearer. We just won't call you Dad."

"Or Uncle, either," Atkins said, with a mock-serious tone.

Hal laughed. "You don't want to be called Uncle Tom?"

"Just Tom. Not Uncle Tom, or Peeping Tom, or Tom Tom, the Piper's Son."

Dane chuckled. "I hadn't even thought of those."

The next day, Saturday, the boys brought in a two-year-old heifer. Atkins noted that they had been scrupulous enough not to put a rope on her. Likewise, he was discreet enough not to look at the brand or ask later what had become of the hide. All he saw was a carcass of hanging beef, which he thought looked just fine. To a fellow who worked in the kitchen, the cold touch of a slab of beef was as assuring as money in the bank.

When Laurel arrived on Sunday, Hal made introductions. "Laurel, this is Tom Atkins. Just call him Tom. He insists. And Tom, this is Laurel Croft. Soon to be Norden."

Atkins liked her right away. She was bright and pretty, with dark hair and rosy cheeks, and a pair of blue-gray eyes that danced. Atkins imagined she was a year or two younger than Hal, although, like young women her age, she seemed as mature as a man five years older. "Pleased to meet you," he said. "I hope you like the ranch."

"Thank you. I know I'm going to love it. And it's nice to meet you, too." She gave a polite smile, then took Hal's arm, and the two of them turned to walk toward the house.

Dane, who had been the first to greet Laurel, stood watching as the young lovers walked away. Then, as if catching himself, he gave a quick look at Atkins and said, "I suppose we can unload the wheel."

That evening, after Hal had taken Laurel to town and had ridden back to the ranch, Atkins served a heap of fried beefsteak and a platter of fried potatoes. As usual, the boys didn't say much as they ate. The knives and forks went clackety-clack, and everyone seemed to have fallen into separate thoughts.

Atkins chewed on a bite of beef. For meat that had been hanging only a day, it tasted fine. "Not a bad little heifer," he said.

Both Hal and Dane gave him an astonished look, and he could tell that at least one if not both had been thinking of Laurel.

Atkins pointed downward with his fork, indicating the steak on his plate. "Good beef, for just being killed yesterday."

"Oh," said Dane. "Uh-huh. It was in good shape for the winter."

Atkins looked at Hal. "I imagine those other folks were happy to get theirs."

"Oh, yeah," Hal said. "Ralph could eat five pounds of it every day, just by himself."

John D. Nesbitt

"Waste not, want not," said Dane. "I'm glad he likes the liver, too."

Hal laughed. "He calls the heart, liver, and kidneys 'gut meat.' "

"The English call it 'organ meat,' " Atkins said. "I've cooked it all for 'em. But don't worry, boys. I won't be makin' any kidney pie at this place."

"Fine by me," Dane answered. "Those Englishmen can have all the mutton, too."

The boys went back to eating, and no one said much for the rest of the meal.

After supper, as Hal helped with the dishes, Atkins said, "That's really a nice girl you've got, Hal."

"She sure is."

"You're a lucky man."

"That's for sure. Sometimes I think I'm too lucky."

"Oh? Why do you say that?"

"Well, that she chose me. Sometimes it seems like girls go in for the rougher type, you know. Like they're more capable or more sure of themselves."

Atkins shook his head. "Maybe some do, but not all."

"Well, no, you're right. And I'm glad Laurel doesn't see things that way. But it's just that sometimes I feel like I'm too lucky, that it's too good to be true."

"Maybe she feels the same way about herself, Hal."

"I don't know."

"I do. You ought to see the two of you. It shows."

The next day, the three men put the wheel on the wagon. Using a six-by-six beam for a lever, Dane and Atkins pushed down on the far end to raise the axle. At each new elevation, Hal reached in and set another block under the axle. Dane told him more than once not to put his head in there, so he had his hat off and his head cocked away as he reached in.

Finally they had the axle high enough, and they slipped the wheel onto the hub.

"Man alive," said Dane when the task was done. "That was a lot of work for a little job like that. You sure miss something as common as a screw jack."

"It was like not having a wheelbarrow the other day," Atkins said. "Have to do everything the hard way."

Dane nodded. "The things you take for granted." He patted the rim of the wheel. "I hope this isn't the best wagon we ever have, but we've got one. We've got a wagon, and we've got a brand."

Atkins looked at the two boys. He felt happy for them, and happy to be part of the NB.

Chapter Three

Atkins held the pitchfork head-up in front of him and observed the ends of the tines. Enough daylight came through the open doorway of the stable to make the bare steel shine. He took off his right glove and touched his index finger to each of the four cold tips. Neither sharp nor blunt, they had enough of a point to go wherever a man poked them. He wondered if, in the course of several years' use, a pitchfork got sharper or duller or stayed about the same. Most of the time, a fellow just poked the fork into hay. But sometimes, to clean off mud or manure, he might run the prongs through dirt. Atkins recalled a time, a few years back, when he had killed a snake with a shotgun and then used a pitchfork to toss the snake into the brush. To clean the

blood off the tines, he ran them through an anthill. It had worked pretty well, but it had left him
wondering whether a thousand swipes through
an anthill would sharpen or dull the points.

He hung the fork on the wall that separated
the stable from the toolshed. Fred Morris had put
up one haystack, and Dane and Atkins hauled a
wagonload of hay each week, backing the wagon
into the stable and leaving it alongside the door
that was still nailed shut. One of the men used
the fork every day to pitch hay to the horses, so
it hung in the stable now, on a pair of nails that
Atkins could see on most afternoons but had to
find with his hand when the daylight was too far
gone. He could see the nails today.

Atkins stepped out into the yard and closed the
stable door. He looked at the little house, dark
and quiet. Soon enough, in a month or so, Hal
would be back with Laurel, and there would be
light at the windows. In the meanwhile, the off-
season was a good time for them to take an unhurried trip. Atkins smiled. It was the time of
year when a lot of young cowpunchers spent
their summer wages on whiskey and women,
when the old guard of cattle country smoked ci-
gars and hobnobbed with cronies in Cheyenne,
and when cooks like himself thought about snow
on the roof and fire in the chimney.

Atkins walked on across the yard and went
into the bunkhouse. The dim interior had a re-

assuring smell to it, a blend of warmth and wood smoke and roasting food. He had left a chunk of beef, along with potatoes and onions, in a pan inside the oven of the cast-iron stove, and the smell of cooking beef brought him pleasure. It seemed as if a man never tired of beef. Atkins had cooked for quite a few outfits, and even when he had been fat-hungry after a week or two of spuds and beans, he didn't care for mutton for more than a day or two. After a week he grew tired of bacon or salt pork as the only meat. He could tell he was tired of a certain kind of meat when the smell of it cooking didn't sharpen the appetite. He didn't ever have that trouble with beef.

Atkins took off his gloves and lit a lantern, then hung his hat and coat on their pegs. He imagined Dane would be riding in at any time, so after putting a can of bacon grease on the stovetop, he set out an enamel pan and started mixing the ingredients for a batch of biscuits. He glanced out the window, and the world seemed to have gotten dark in short order. That was winter, he thought, when a fellow stood in a lighted room and looked out into the gathering dusk. He had just had his birthday—January 24—a few days earlier, and when that time of the winter came around, he could tell the days were getting a couple of minutes longer each day. Still, the dark seemed to close in fast.

He went to the stove for the bacon grease, which was melted now and usable for the biscuit dough. As he poured the grease into the dry mix in the pan, he heard horse hooves on the hard ground outside. That would be Dane. No one else had been by the ranch since Hal left, and Dane had taken to riding out each afternoon when the weather was tolerable. Atkins thought he heard the stable door open; then he started clacking at the dough with a spoon, and he didn't hear anything from outside.

He made drop biscuits, pushing each gob of dough off the spoon with his right index finger. He portioned out an even dozen, six in each pie tin, and was just putting them in the oven when Dane came into the bunkhouse.

After taking off his hat and coat and getting cleaned up, Dane sat at the table and rolled a cigarette.

"See anything?"

Dane yawned. "Not to mention." A thoughtful look came to his face as he lit his cigarette. "I thought we might go into town tomorrow."

Atkins paused for a second. Today was Tuesday. Young fellows like Dane liked to go into town on Saturday, but Atkins supposed it didn't matter much in the middle of the winter. A ride to town would help shake off the doldrums. "Sounds good enough," he said. "I could use a few things."

Supper went by without much conversation. With Hal gone, Dane wasn't much of a talker most of the time anyway, and when he had his sleeves rolled up and a knife and fork in action, he said even less. When the meal was finished he brought out his ledgers, then rolled a smoke, lit it, and started turning pages. It was a routine he went through every evening, even though there weren't a great many new details to add from one week to the next. Atkins imagined it was Dane's way of not being idle while someone else was working, in addition to staying attentive to the business end of running a ranch.

The next morning, after breakfast and chores, Dane and Atkins got ready to go to town. Dane saddled one of the NB horses, a black, while Atkins saddled his own horse. He could ride ranch horses if he wanted, but his two horses hadn't gotten much exercise of late, so he thought the stocky brown horse could use a day's work.

It was a calm morning, not very cold but not warm either. Thin, high clouds filled the sky, and pale sunlight lit up the plains. The two horses kept up a brisk, even walk and brought the riders into the town of Farris before the sun had reached its high point for the day.

The main street ran east and west, with most of the businesses of any account clustered along a four-block stretch. As Atkins looked up and down the street, he thought the town was pretty slow for a late morning in the middle of the week. A few ranch wagons and saddle horses stood here and there in front of businesses, but nothing was in motion at the moment. In the middle of the second block on the left, someone sat on a bench in front of Chapman's Mercantile. No one else was on the sidewalks or in the street.

When the two riders were still a block away from the mercantile, Dane spoke. "I need to take a little ride for a few blocks on my own. I'll meet you in the store after a while."

Atkins looked at him and nodded. Whatever Dane was up to was his business.

Dane let Atkins ride ahead, then turned left behind the brown horse. Atkins gave a quarter turn with his head and saw Dane and the black horse head down the side street.

Atkins rode on and turned in at the mercantile. Chapman's store had grown to include two separate businesses—a general store that carried food and dry goods, and a hardware store that carried work items and furniture. Although Chapman did seem casual and unhurried in procuring merchandise for his customers when he didn't have it on hand, Atkins thought he was aggressive in his own way. Having bought up and combined two separate businesses and the only ones of their kind in town, he commanded at least his share of the town's commerce.

Just before dismounting, Atkins waved to the

person sitting on the bench in front of the store. As he had thought, it was Ev Mason, who spent the middle part of bright winter days squinting into the sun. At this time of year the sun was far enough south that buildings on the north side of a street caught and reflected a fair amount of warmth. As usual, Mason was bundled up and had his crutches leaning against the bench.

Atkins swung down from the saddle, tied his horse to the hitching rail, and stepped up onto the sidewalk. "Well, hello, Ev. How are you doin' today?"

"No damn good, Tom. But that's not anything new. And yourself?"

"Not too bad." Atkins looked at the pasty face, the pale blue eyes, the drab brown hair that stuck out beneath the fur cap. "Turned out to be a halfway decent day. Not a bad day to ride into town."

"Could be," Mason answered, looking beyond Atkins as if he was assessing the value of the day's sunshine. "One day's about like the next, though."

Atkins nodded and turned down the corners of his mouth. "I suppose so." He glanced at Mason's left leg, which ended right below the knee and had the trouser leg tucked up behind. Conversation with Mason was like this, weighted with a sense of obligation to lend an ear for a few minutes.

Mason turned his pale eyes toward Atkins.

"Every day is just another one you're not goin' to see again, that's what."

Atkins nodded again. Mason was about the same age as he was, but bad luck with his health had left him with a jaded attitude. "I'd say you're right, Ev."

"I'd say I am. Be glad you can still ride a horse, Tom." Mason leaned his head back, opened his mouth, and took in a breath of air. "Life only gives you half a chance, you know."

Atkins swallowed. Even when the conversation seemed to be going through its routine, he couldn't dismiss the parts that made him uncomfortable. "I guess some of us just get more than we deserve."

Mason shook his head. "It's all the same. You take what you get. We all do."

Atkins shifted his weight as he stood on the board sidewalk. "I guess that's all we can do."

"Uh-huh. And the crookedest son of a bitch in the world dies in bed with a hard-on at eighty."

"Seems to work that way." The conversation was smoothing out again.

"You just take what you get. And if you end up not bein' fit to do anything but fling your piss on an anthill, you call it good."

"Uh-huh."

Mason smiled. "Just a few happy words to help pass the time."

41

Atkins couldn't help smiling back. "It always works."

"Go ahead, Tom. Go on in. Don't let me keep you here." Mason motioned with his head.

Atkins winked. "You'll be around as long as any of us, Ev. You're too damn bitter not to."

Mason shook his head. "I'm too damn sweet. That's the trouble."

Atkins went into the store, where as the tinkle of the bell died away he paused for a moment to let his eyes adjust to the dim interior. An aisle led from the doorway to the back of the store. No one stood at the counter, so Atkins had a clear view of a set of deer antlers, four points on each side, hanging on the wall behind the cash box. Atkins looked to either side of the aisle as he walked into the interior of the store.

A woman's voice at his right stopped him. "May I help you find something?"

He turned and recognized Mrs. Chapman, the storekeeper's wife. "Oh, hello," he said. He had a sense of something being out of place, but in his first glance he saw that she looked as always, full-bodied and well-dressed. She was in her middle to late twenties and starting to put on a little weight, but she hadn't given in to the role of dull matron. Feminine vitality lurked beneath the wool exterior, and her blue eyes flashed. Atkins had the feeling that she was afraid of losing her appeal and practiced it when she could, even with him.

"What brings you to town by yourself on a day like this?" She gave a mild backward toss to her head, and her blond hair, which was cut to a length below her ears, made a brief wavy motion and came to rest again.

Atkins knew that if there was anything smoldering it was not for him, but his sense of gallantry responded to her playful tone. "Dwindling supplies in the pantry," he said. "But if the truth be known, I didn't come by myself."

Mrs. Chapman did not answer but rather stood with an open expression, a half-smile, on her face. Then, when the moment seemed to have passed for her to answer, she said, "Oh."

"Uh-huh. Dane and I rode in together."

She gave a slight tilt to her head as she nodded.

"He went off on some errand, but I'm sure he'll be along in a few minutes."

"Well," she said, "we can get started on your order in the meanwhile."

A movement on Atkins's left caught his attention. It was Chapman, the storekeeper, who stood in the center aisle.

"Hello, Tom," he said.

"Hello, Al." Atkins took in the clear eyes, neat mustache, and clean complexion. The man was not imposing, but he had a self-assured air about him as he took up the center of the aisle. He was the picture of a robust storekeeper, with his gabardine coat, clean white shirt, and spreading waistcoat. Like other men of his class, he carried his weight like a privilege.

Chapman looked at his wife. "Ida, dear, how would it be if I took care of Mr. Atkins?"

She smiled. "Certainly."

Chapman turned to Atkins with a jaunty smile. "Division of labor. When both of us are on hand, I don't tend to ladies' ailments, and she doesn't cut bacon."

From the corner of his eye, Atkins saw Mrs. Chapman walk away. It occurred to him that he had not seen her in the store all that often. That was what had seemed out of place. The last time he had seen her was at Hal's wedding party, and he had been in the store a couple of times since then. He looked at Chapman and did not sense that his momentary gallantry had aroused any concern in the man. "A good plan," he bantered. "If I ever get so lucky as to have a wife, I'll remember the lesson of Jack Sprat."

Chapman pursed his mustache over a suppressed smile. Although he was a few years younger than Atkins, he had the deportment of a man who had arrived at the age of worldly wisdom. Nodding, he said, "May you be so blessed."

Atkins thought Chapman might consider matrimony a mixed blessing, but from the briskness Atkins had felt in the woman's presence, he imagined there might be an element of pride. If a man had something he had to look out for, it might be something to be proud of having, if only because other men envied him. Atkins felt a smile come to his face as he said, "Thanks."

"Well," said Chapman, settling back into his role of accommodating storekeeper, "what can we fix you up with today?"

Atkins couldn't resist another touch with the spur. "Would you like to get your hands greasy with the bacon first, or shall we go through the beans and flour and dried apples and canned tomatoes?"

"Let's do the dry things first." Chapman turned and walked back toward the counter.

Following, Atkins said, "Let's have five pounds of beans and ten pounds of flour, five pounds of dried apples, and half a dozen cans of tomatoes."

Chapman spoke over his left shoulder. "That's not very much."

"Well, you know, Hal's gone, so it's just Dane and me."

"Oh. Uh-huh."

"And we just came in on our horses, so we don't have room for any large amounts."

Chapman stopped at the counter, turned, and sniffed. "Oh, I see." He picked up a scoop from the counter and lifted the tray from the scales, then moved to a tub of dry beans that sat on top of an upright wooden keg. "You know," he said, with his back turned, "I don't usually sell flour in any amount less than a twenty-five-pound bag." He dumped the first scoop of beans into the tray and turned halfway to face Atkins. "If you don't mind."

"No, that should be all right."

Chapman finished measuring out the beans and weighing them, then went on to the dried apples and canned tomatoes. He set all of the items on the counter along with the bag of flour. "Now for the bacon," he said, turning to pass through a doorway in the partition that separated the front part of the store from the back. The opening was below and to the right of the deer antlers.

As Chapman came back through the doorway with a large slab of bacon in his hands, the bell on the front door tinkled. He gave a sharp glance and then looked at Atkins. "You said five pounds, didn't you?"

"Actually, I didn't, but that sounds fine." Atkins turned to see Dane walking down the aisle.

"Findin' everything, Tom?"

"Just right."

"Good." Dane glanced at the man carving the bacon. "Hello, Al," he said, and then looked around the store.

Chapman looked up and back down as he answered. "Hello, Dane."

46

Dane looked at Atkins and said, "There's another thing I want." He turned to his right and raised his head so that his hat brim went up. "I'll ask over here." His boot heels sounded on the wooden floor as he walked behind Atkins.

Mrs. Chapman's voice, clear and pleasant, carried all the way to the counter as she asked Dane what he needed.

"Bag balm," he answered.

Chapman stuck his knife in the chopping block, then gave a firm look at his wife as he wiped his hands on a towel. "It's with the horse liniment and boluses. In a square can."

Atkins watched as the storekeeper wrapped the bacon in brown paper once and then twice.

"Damn. I forgot to weight it first."

"No matter," said Atkins. "Weigh it that way is fine."

Dane's boot heels sounded as his steps came back to the counter. He set the pale green can next to the other items.

Chapman's eyebrows flickered as he looked over the assortment of articles. Atkins imagined he was wondering what the balm was for. An outfit like the NB would not likely have a milk cow.

"This cold weather really does it," Chapman said without looking up as he added the prices on a slip of paper.

"Sure does," Dane answered. "And the way

47

Tom makes me wash the dishes day and night, my hands crack wide open."

Atkins laughed, quick and short.

Chapman smiled. "Is that right, Tom?"

"That's right. And he used up all the mutton tallow I had on hand."

Chapman clucked as he turned the slip of paper around and slid it toward Dane.

Out on the sidewalk, Atkins asked Dane if he had anything else to do in town.

"No hurry to go straight back," Dane said, looking up and down the street. "We can leave these things in the stable with the horses for a little while, and make good use of our time."

Atkins did not try to guess what Dane had in mind, or he would have been wondering since they first came into town. Instead, he just went along as they left their supplies in the stable and put up the horses for a while.

Back on the street, looking east at the town, Dane said, "Let's try the Elkhorn."

Atkins pushed out his lower lip and nodded. The Elkhorn lay on the same side of the street as Chapman's Mercantile and two blocks farther east. The front part of the saloon dedicated itself to serving drinks and hosting card games, while the back parlor provided a place for men to meet women. Atkins thought he could take care of himself in such a place.

Atkins and Dane walked along the sidewalk,

Atkins on the outside. He saw that the center of town still had little activity. A single horse stood tied in front of Chapman's store, and the bench in front was empty. Atkins absorbed the faint warmth of the sunlight and felt relaxed, with nothing more pressing than the thought of what he might order to drink.

The door of Chapman's store opened, and as the tinkling of the bell faded, the storekeeper's voice carried out onto the winter air, not in distinct words but in the hearty tone of good fellowship. A voice answered, and out of the doorway stepped a figure that Atkins recognized and then identified. The gray wool coat, the dark, broad-brimmed hat, and the shifting brown eyes coalesced into the person of Orvus Fey.

The man in the charcoal-colored hat stopped short to let the other two men pass. He smiled and said, "How d'ye'do?" and showed his teeth as before.

Dane and Atkins returned the greeting and walked on. Atkins felt the man's gaze follow them, and from the spare exchange he sensed that there had been an air of restraint on Fey's part—condescension, perhaps, but not a lack of interest.

Once inside the Elkhorn, Atkins thought again about what he would drink. When Dane ordered whiskey, Atkins did the same. He thought it was a little early to be drinking much at all, especially without having had noon dinner, so he took a small sip of the liquor.

"Looks like that fellow Fey is a man of leisure like we are," he said, turning to his right.

"I suppose." Dane was looking at the mirror in back of the bar.

"Do you get a funny feeling from him?"

Dane wrinkled his nose. "Not so much."

"Well, I do."

Dane gave a quarter-turn to look at Atkins. "He barely knows us."

"I know, but I feel like there's something." Atkins gave a tilt to his glass to set the whiskey swirling, then looked at Dane. "If it's not personal on his part, do you think his boss has something against you?"

Dane shrugged. "Oh, he might. He tried to get Morris to sell the place to him."

"Oh, uh-huh."

"Yeah. But Fred thought he'd rather sell it to a couple of his own men." Dane's left eyebrow went up. "Of course, he owed us both a season's worth of wages, so he might have thought he was saving something there."

"Hmmm."

Dane reached inside his coat and brought out his tobacco and papers. "But there's not much he can do about it, unless we go broke." Dane pushed out his lips. "And that could happen to anyone, him included."

As Dane rolled his cigarette and lit it, Atkins could tell that the young man had something else on his mind—something that weighed more than a curt greeting from a newcomer. Atkins swirled his drink again and took another little sip.

"Chapman was his usual self," he said.

Dane turned to look at Atkins. "How do you mean?"

"Oh, just in the way he acts. Like he's there to please you, but you have to do things his way."

Dane blew a stream of smoke through his nostrils. "The rooster of his own little dunghill."

Knowing he had hit on something, Atkins added up a few details—Dane's sidestep purchase in the store, his earlier errand, the sharp looks of the storekeeper, the earlier incident of the hinges. Thinking back to Hal's wedding party, he remembered noticing for the first time that Mrs. Chapman had a quick eye. It must have landed on the vigorous young cowboy a while before that.

"He looks like he's putting on weight."

Dane took a slow drag and exhaled. "He could get as fat as a hog, for all I care." He looked at his cigarette and then said, "A good square kick in the ass is what he needs."

"It wouldn't hurt his business," Atkins said.

Dane put away his first drink and called for a second, and not long after that he asked for another. Although he didn't say much, his humor

51

did not seem to be improving. Atkins asked if he wanted to get something to eat, and he said not yet.

When Dane finished his third glass of whiskey, he looked at Atkins, who was still nursing his first drink, and said, "Why don't we go to the parlor?"

Atkins looked at Dane's face, sulky but relaxed from the liquor. "Might be good medicine," he said. He tossed off the rest of his drink.

Once in the parlor, the men ordered drinks and sat on a cloth-covered sofa. A buxom lady in her mid-thirties asked if they were interested in anyone in particular, and they answered no. She left the room, to be replaced a minute later with a row of four young women. The one on the left, a dark-haired girl of about twenty, did not look at Atkins. She seemed to catch Dane's eye right away, for he rose with his drink in his hand and walked out of the room with her. The other three, all in their mid-twenties and a little plump, let their eyes rove back and forth as Atkins looked at his choices. After a couple of minutes, his eyes met those of a blond girl in a red dress. She was not very pretty, but her blue eyes were friendly. When he nodded at her, the other two girls left. She came and sat next to him on the couch.

She asked his name and said hers was Dolly. Atkins knew that girls who turned to this line of work sometimes took on a new name, and he wondered if her name was the same as when she grew up in her parents' house. She had a soft, inviting way about her as she put her hand on his leg, just above the knee, and asked what he liked.

Feeling himself respond in the right way, he said he liked girls and hadn't outgrown them yet.

She said she had a nice place for a boy like him, and she asked if he would like to see it.

He said he would, and then she was leading him by the hand down a dim hallway. She stopped at a door, tapped on the panel, and then turned the handle. She led him into the chilly room, where she lit a lamp and then turned to him.

"You know I have to look at you first," she said, resting her hand on his belt.

"Sure," he answered. He leaned toward a dresser and set his glass of whiskey on it. Then he helped her make her inspection.

They wasted no time getting undressed in the cold room, and then they were together under the single wool blanket and cotton sheet that covered the bed.

She was soft and sweet, with kind hands and gentle motion. Atkins had not been with a woman in quite a while, but all of the intervening time vanished, and it seemed as if he had never done anything but this.

A little while later, as he lay with his head on the pillow, she asked him what was so funny.

"Oh, not much," he said. "I just remembered something I said a while back."

"Today?"

"No, a few months ago. When these boys hired me to go to work for them."

Her touch was soft on his upper arm. "What was that?"

"I told 'em I could still rope." He turned to her and smiled. "I guess I can."

Her blue eyes were still friendly, at a moment when some girls would already be back up and dressing. "I'd say you rope mighty fine," she said.

He nodded, still smiling. He knew it was her job to say nice things like that, but he also knew she wouldn't have said it in such a nice way if she didn't want him to come back again sometime.

Dane was waiting at the bar when Atkins made his way back out to the saloon. He had a drink in front of him, and his voice had a slur as he spoke. "How did you do?"

"Oh, all right. And you?"

"Good enough, I guess."

"That was a nice-enough-looking girl you had."

"Oh, sure." Dane turned down the corners of

his mouth. "But that's all I can get. The kind that just wants to make a few dollars."

Atkins shrugged. "There aren't many others around here."

"Well, there are, but they're married to the wrong kind."

Atkins felt a little jolt of fear. "Speaking principally of fat-asses, I hope."

Dane's answer was quick. "Speaking *only* of fat-asses." He picked up his glass and rotated it by the base, then looked at Atkins. "I'm sick of this whole town already. Shall we get something to eat and then get the hell out?"

"Might as well." Atkins watched him toss off the rest of his drink. It was too bad the other medicine hadn't done Dane a little more good.

Chapter Four

Atkins swung the ax in a hard, downward stroke, causing the chips to fly as the steel blade sank into the log. The jolt felt good. The muscles in his arms had warmed up, and he felt the strength flowing in them. He swung again and again, making a good bite each time and rotating the log after every three or four cuts. When he thought the notch was deep enough all the way around, he swung the ax down straight and hit the log square. It separated. He took one of the two lengths, set it upright, and cleaved it in two with another hard stroke. He set up the remaining piece and split it the same way.

For as much as this wood was hard and resisted the ax, it burned fast. Atkins had split the two thickest sections so that the pieces would all burn down at about the same time and leave him an adequate bed of coals for making biscuits.

With his wooden pothook he lifted the Dutch oven that was squatting in the fire pit, and he set it at the edge, still in the pit but away from the center. He lifted the lid, got a satisfactory whiff of bacon and beans, and covered the pot again. Crouching, he laid the split pieces of firewood on the coals, then laid the narrower pieces on top. He took off his hat and fanned the embers until a flame sprang up.

Atkins settled back in his crouch and watched the fire take hold. He thought the dead tree might have been some kind of an elm. It burned like elm and had a similar shape, but he didn't know how it would have gotten here unless someone planted it. He had used this same fire pit the season before, when he ran the wagon for the Dupré outfit, and he remembered the campsite with its supply of deadfall. But he didn't know if there had ever been a dwelling at this spot along the creek.

When he was sure the fire had caught, he stood up and went to the tailgate of the chuck wagon, where he took out an enamel mixing bowl and started putting together a batch of biscuit dough. He glanced at the fire, then back at his work. When the dough was ready, he got out his second Dutch oven and hung it on the tripod to heat it up. He took his swab stick from its place by the chuck box, dipped the swab end into his can of bacon grease, and smeared the inside of the cast-iron vessel. After a couple of minutes, when the smoke began to wisp up from the hot greasy metal, Atkins used the pothook to lift the Dutch oven from its place over the fire and set it next to the wagon. When the fire had burned almost all the way to coals, he set the pot in the middle of the glowing embers.

After a few more minutes he put his hand over the pot and counted. He didn't have to pull his hand away until he counted to eight, so he let the oven heat some more. For biscuits he liked a fire hot enough that he had to pull his hand away after four seconds, or six at the most. He checked it again, and it had heated up to five, so he started spooning in the dough. He set the gobs in a ring around the inside circumference of the pot, and then he dropped a gob in the middle. With his pothook he set the lid on top, then gave it a quarter turn to settle it snug. He set the pothook to rest on a stone and took out his watch. With a fire like this that wasn't very hot, the biscuits would take about fifteen minutes or a little more.

Atkins had the good feeling of having things in order. Cooking for a crew of four, as he was doing now, was not all that hard, but it still required organization, timing, and some hot, hurried work.

He looked over at the horse herd, where

Tincher and Diego stood talking. They had just tied up the ends of the rope corral, and he imagined they were waiting for him to beat the triangle. Hal and Dane, on horseback, were visible on the other side of the corral, where they were looking over the remuda. To Atkins it looked like they had about twenty head, so the horse gather was going well.

The Norden boys had hired Tincher and Diego a week earlier, in preparation for spring roundup. The crew was taking a couple of days to gather the horses, which they would then take back to the ranch. They would sort the horses and work with them until the twenty-fifth of May, when they would join in with a few other small outfits for the spring roundup.

Atkins saw Tincher glance in the direction of the chuck wagon and then back at Diego. Tincher was always looking at something, it seemed. On several occasions in the last week, Atkins had felt the man's eye on him, and when he had looked up or around, Tincher was just turning his gaze. It happened back at the ranch, when Atkins would go to fetch the ax or bring in firewood, and he felt it out here on the range, when he was rustling up grub. And it had happened just a little while earlier, when he was starting to cut firewood.

Atkins wondered if Tincher liked to know everybody's routines or if he just had the habit of watching. Whatever the case, he took in plenty. Atkins had felt his own blood rise when he saw Tincher staring at Laurel, but he made himself mind his own business. If Tincher went too far, even in gawking, he would have both the Norden boys to deal with; so in spite of his urge to club Tincher with a length of stove wood, Atkins gritted his teeth.

He also wondered if Tincher's habit of watching came from his having only one eye that worked. His left eye was what some people called a walleye—a dull eye that didn't track with the good eye or show any reaction. Atkins didn't think that was the whole explanation, as Tincher's habit of observation was connected to another one. He had the tendency to insinuate himself into other people's affairs by way of questions and comments as well as by watching. If it were just a matter of arithmetic, of having to look twice as long to see as much as the average person would see with two eyes, Atkins imagined he would have developed an ability to do it without seeming like a busybody. But he didn't.

Atkins went about straightening up his utensils and ingredients. He washed the mixing bowl and pitched the water out beyond the edge of the campsite. Next he got the coffeepot ready. After checking his watch, he used the wooden pothook to lift the lid on the Dutch oven. The biscuits were brown around the sides and on the peaks. He lowered the lid, set the pothook back on its rock, and went for the triangle. Holding it up by its leather thong, he clanged the iron bar around the inside of the triangle. The notes rang sweet and clear on the prairie, sending out a song that every ranch hand knew. When Atkins was done sounding the call, he held the bar and the triangle in his right hand and used his left to still the vibrations.

Atkins lifted the Dutch oven from the coals and set it on the ground, where he uncovered it and dug out the biscuits with a spoon. Setting the tin plate of biscuits on the tailgate, he grabbed his shovel, raked the coals together, and hung the coffeepot right above them. Then with the pothook he lifted the lid off the beans, and chuck was ready.

Tincher and Diego came sauntering in, with the two brothers not far behind. Hal and Dane dismounted a few yards out, walked their horses in, and tied them to the front wheel of the wagon.

"Best part of the day," said Tincher as he grabbed a plate and spoon.

Atkins noticed the bad eye, with the white blur at the bottom of the iris, not quite enough to make it a chalk-eye. He told himself, again, that it was something the man hadn't chosen and therefore not something to be held against him.

Diego, the horse wrangler, was next. He was

61

of average height, maybe an inch or two shorter than Tincher. He had a clear, tan complexion and large brown eyes. He smiled at Atkins as he waited his turn, plate and spoon in hand.

Stooped over the beans and with his back to the wagon, Tincher spoke. "Looks like yer kind of grub, Dago." He stood up and turned with his steaming plate in his hands. "Beans." He grinned, showing a gap next to his front left tooth, and then moved aside to find a place to sit down.

Atkins looked around the camp and tried to ignore Tincher's remark, but it irked him all the same. It brought back the way the man was, always ready with a comment that intruded, always ready with a smile and a laugh. Atkins looked at him as he shoveled in the grub. Every working man deserved to eat, and he couldn't begrudge him that. But because of the way Tincher chose to act, Atkins had come to dislike the very details of the man—the hatband with silver conchos, the unwashed neckerchief that did not cover the whelks on his neck, the rough, unshaven face, and the dull eye.

Tincher looked up. "Good grub, Tom."

"Thanks. I hope there's plenty."

Tincher smiled, not quite showing the gap this time. "Me too."

When the men had finished eating, Dane and Tincher rolled cigarettes and lit them. Hal drank from his coffee cup and didn't say much, as usual. An after-dinner laziness had set in around the camp, with the warm sun overhead and everyone having taken on a good feed. The horses were quiet, and there wasn't a herd of bawling cattle nearby.

Tincher had been rattling on about his adventures this past winter in St. Louis. He was telling about the dirty hotels and crooked gambling, and the others were paying minimal attention. In what seemed like a deliberate motion, he sat up straight and flicked a dead match into the fire pit.

"I'll tell ya," he said. "Sometimes what you think is unusual turns out to be just plain normal." He looked around, and having gotten a little more attention, he continued. "Now you've probably noticed that yer Mexican women are generally a little shorter, on the average, than yer white women." He paused to take a drag on his cigarette. "But the shortest woman I ever laid up with was a white woman. Right there in St. Louis, workin' the dives with the rest of 'em. You know, the crib girls come in all kinds there. So anyway, I thought a midget would be somethin' interestin' to try. Come to find out, it wasn't all that different. Lay 'em down, and their height doesn't mean much at all."

Dane looked at Atkins and then at Tincher. "How do you keep from gettin' the clap?"

Tincher, holding his cigarette away from his

mouth, swayed his head to the left to look at Dane. "I only had it once, and it went away by itself."

Dane looked at Atkins, who gave a very small frown. *To hell with him,* Atkins thought. He had told Dane, after the day in town, how to protect against that sort of thing. Save the last drink of whiskey and give the little feller a dousing. But he didn't feel like telling Tincher. Let him get the clap and think it was no trouble.

Dane gave the faintest of nods and said, "I guess you've been lucky."

Tincher smiled and showed the gap in his teeth. "If you saw some of the women I've been with, you'd know I was damn lucky."

A few minutes later, Dane stood up and tossed his cigarette butt into the fire. The others got up also, and everyone went back to work. Diego stayed with the horse herd while Tincher, Dane, and Hal rode out to look for more.

All the horses in the herd were geldings, with no foals or strays. The boys brought in only those horses that carried Fred Morris's Bar-M brand. Having worked for Fred, the boys knew the horses and had a good idea of how many they should find. According to Dane, there were another half dozen or so to be brought in.

While the riders were out hunting horses, Diego took his rifle from the wagon and went up the creek a ways. Atkins heard the gun pop a few times, and after a while Diego came back carrying a couple of dead rabbits by the ears. He laid them on the ground near the wagon.

"What do you think about cookin' these?"

Atkins looked at the two animals and nodded. He didn't like to eat rabbit much later in the year than this, but the weather hadn't warmed up all that much yet. "It should be all right. If you clean 'em, I'll cook 'em."

As the horse wrangler was also the cook's helper, Diego was used to doing what Atkins told him. He put his rifle back in the wagon, then took a pail to the creek and brought it back dripping, half full of water. He picked up the rabbits and carried them and the pail to his place by the horse herd.

Half an hour later, he came back with two clean pink carcasses half floating in the water.

"Looks good, Diego. I'll flour 'em and fry 'em and cook 'em in gravy."

Diego smiled. "Anything else?"

"Not right now—no, wait. Actually, I could use some more firewood. I was going to go get some, but if I need to cut up these rabbits and take care of them, I could use some help. Drag me back a few good-sized branches like the one I cut up before dinner, and I can whack 'em into pieces. Don't stay away from those horses too long, though."

Diego nodded and went back up the creek

where he had gone hunting. Atkins watched him walk. He went right at his work and didn't dawdle. He was a good, solid lad, the kind that caught on well to the way someone wanted things done. He might make a good cowpuncher some day, which was what every horse wrangler wanted. Meanwhile, he did well at any job he was given.

For supper, Atkins heated the leftover beans and made two batches of biscuits, so the rabbit meat and gravy was something extra. Two little cottontail rabbits wouldn't go far with five hungry men, but they made a good side dish. As the meal got under way, Atkins was not surprised to hear Tincher make a comment about the rabbit.

"Can't say I'd want to pick these little bones every day," said Tincher, sucking at his teeth. "But this gravy's not too bad."

"Tastes fine to me," said Dane.

Tincher used his knife to pick at the teeth on the right side of his mouth. "Yer folks eat a lot of this kinda meat, Dago?"

"We eat the normal things you can hunt or raise yourself."

"Oh, uh-huh. You-all eat a lot of sheep and goat?"

Diego took a bite off a front leg he had just separated from its rib cage. "That's right."

Tincher sucked at his teeth again. "I thought I'd heard that. I've never ate goat."

66

"It's good enough."

"I ate mutton once. I couldn't eat it again. It's too greezy. But I guess you people go in for that."

Diego looked up. "Go in for what?"

"Greezy food. You-all cook with a lot of lard. Isn't that right?"

Diego shrugged. "I guess so. Some people more than others."

"And mutton too. Sheepherders eat it seven days a week. The smell's enough to gag me." Tincher shook his head. "Of course, sheepherders are used to the smell. Hell, they stick their nose between a sheep's legs to bite the balls off."

Diego tossed a rabbit bone into the fire but said nothing.

"Have you ever done that, Dago?"

Dane cut in. "Mike, why don't you dry up on that subject? We're eating, you know."

Tincher sniffed and then cleared his throat. "No harm intended. It's just that I've seen a lot of Mexicans that were sheepherders."

"I'm sure you have," Dane said, "but if you could dry up on that, the rest of us could enjoy our supper."

Tincher's answer was quick. "Fine by me. I was thinkin' of havin' a little more myself." He looked at Atkins and smiled. "Good grub, Tom. All of it."

Atkins laughed at Tincher's quick adjustment. "Be careful what you say. We had a cook one

67

time, when I first started out at ranch work, and
he cooked up the most god-awful slumgullions.
But you had to tell him you liked it, or he'd get
mad. And a mad cook is worse than a bad one.
So he'd cook up something you could hardly
choke down, and everybody would say it tasted
fine, and he'd say good. Then he'd turn around
and fix the same mess for two or three more
days."

Hal looked up from his meal. "What was the
worst thing he cooked?"

"Well, he was Irish, so he was big on spuds.
They were all right. But whenever he could get
cabbage, he'd boil up a feed of that, too. The
boys didn't eat it up right away, so he usually had
some left over. Then the next day he'd fry it in
whatever grease he had on hand."

Hal laughed. "The boys should have caught
on, and eaten all the cabbage the first night."

"It would have been the thing to do. But I
don't think any of us ever thought of it."

Hal smiled. "You see? We're ready for you
now."

Atkins laughed. "We'd better not make it a
contest. I think I could make some of those
things he served up."

At midmorning of the next day, Hal brought in
a young steer on the end of his rope, a yearling
with a knobby knee on the front left. "Tom," he

said, "we're going to do something unusual. We're going to kill one of our own beef."

Atkins lifted his head in half a nod. "Uh-huh. I won't tell anyone."

"Good." Hal smiled and went on. "We might as well do it here. You can haul him back in the wagon faster than he can walk."

Atkins looked at the young steer. It was neither fat nor lean. "How much of it do you think we'll be able to eat before we go on roundup?"

"Oh, most of it. I'll take some of it in to Ralph and Susie. You know Laurel's going to stay with them for the time that we're on roundup."

"Oh, that should be fine, then. Diego and I can take care of it."

Atkins tied the animal to the front wagon wheel, then took off Hal's rope so he could coil it up.

When Hal had ridden away, Atkins went to the wagon and took his six-shooter out of his duffel bag. He thought Diego might like to do the job, so he called him over and told him what they had to do. Handing him the gun, he said, "I'm going to lead him a little ways away from the wagon, and when I stand back, get ready. Wait till he looks straight at you, and then give it to him between the eyes."

Diego nodded and took the revolver in his right hand. Atkins untied the rope from the wagon wheel and led the steer out on the other side of the wagon from the horse herd. Stopping, he looked back at Diego. The young man carried the six-shooter, pointing down, until he came within a couple of yards of the steer. Holding the gun out at arm's length, he waited as Atkins had told him to do, and when the steer looked at him with both eyes straight on, he fired.

The steer left the ground with all four feet at once, then collapsed on its left side.

"Good work," said Atkins. He went and got a knife from the tailgate and handed it to Diego. "Let's go ahead and bleed him."

Diego traded the gun for the knife and moved in for the next part of the job. Atkins could see he had done some of this work before and was not squeamish.

By noon they had the animal skinned, cleaned, and quartered. Diego dragged the offal into the sagebrush away from camp, and then he helped Atkins set the four quarters on a canvas sheet on the ground, in the shade of the wagon. Atkins was pleased with the neat, clean job.

At dinnertime, Dane said they had all the horses he and Hal expected to gather up. "I think there might be one or two more out there, but they might be winterkill or who knows what. We'll take these in."

Atkins nodded. He had figured they would be going back in, or they would have waited to kill the steer.

Dane looked at Tincher. "Mike, you can ride in with Hal and me. We'll let Hal go first, and I think all these horses should follow all right. They've all been there before. You and I can ride drag. It should go pretty fast."

"Done it before," Tincher said.

"Good." Dane turned to the wrangler. "Diego, you can help Tom get everything loaded up and then ride in with him."

When dinner was over, Tincher came to stand by Atkins and Diego by the tailgate. He wouldn't have been much taller than either of them in stocking feet, but he wore boots with thick heels, and they gave him a bit of a swagger when he stood close.

"Dago," he said, "you make sure you lift the heavy end of all those pieces of beef."

Diego, who might have had the reasonable thought that there was one man on the crew he did not have to take orders from, did not answer. He just looked at Atkins.

Silence hung in the air for a second or two. Atkins had his own thoughts but drew in his lower lip and said nothing. Then Dane's voice came from the fire pit.

"Don't worry about Tom," he said. "He's got more beans than you think."

Tincher shrugged. "Just thought I'd mention it."

Atkins watched him walk away, the red pus-

71

tules showing above the dirty bandanna. Tincher was a good-enough hand, it seemed, but he was bound to get tiresome in the next few months. He seemed to think that being on horseback was the only important work, that riding hard and taking falls was heroic. If someone wasn't doing that, then he probably never did or never could, and whatever else he was doing was servant work. *To hell with him,* Atkins thought. One of these days, sooner or later, if there was any fairness in the world, Tincher would take a good hard fall. Whether it was an outlaw horse or something of his own doing, it could change his outlook a bit. Then he might not be so hard to take.

Dane's voice came again from the firepit, where he was standing with Hal. "Say, Tom. What would you think of building up this fire?"

"I suppose I could. What have you got in mind?"

"We haven't branded anything yet with our new brand."

Atkins looked around. "You didn't bring in any more cattle, did you?"

"No, and we really shouldn't brand anything like that until we put in with the other outfits." Dane looked at Hal and then back at Atkins. "We thought we could burn our brand into each side of the chuck box."

Atkins glanced at the box that rose up above

the sideboards of the wagon. "That should be all right." He looked back at the fire pit. "Let me get my things out of the way, and we'll build her up."

He built a quick fire with plenty of small pieces, and before long he had a small heap of coals. Hal poked the end of the iron into the glowing mound, which opened and looked like the red center of a furnace. He waited, kneeling, for a couple of minutes, and then he pulled out the hot iron and handed it to Dane.

Atkins enjoyed the moment. Tincher was off saddling a fresh horse, and Diego was minding the ropes on the corral. Here were the boys, acting like boys, putting their brand on the chuck box. And yet it was serious, also, to see two brothers who were hoping to build a ranch. They had chosen to do this on their own. They had worked together, saved together, and gotten the NB brand together. It was something to appreciate.

Chapter Five

Atkins slipped the bit into the dun horse's mouth and drew the headstall up over the ears. As he did so, his left hand let go of the side pieces and took hold of the reins that hung down. Someone, long before Atkins bought the used bit in a saddle shop in Cheyenne, had taken the trouble to fashion the side pieces, or shanks, in the shape of a woman's leg. Looking at the bit, Atkins appreciated the artistry, anonymous now, of a craftsman who put a little grace into a plain piece of steel. It did not change the function of the bit, though. Atkins knew, as would any horse that had it in its mouth, that it was for control.

Atkins tightened the front cinch, then led the horse out of the stable and into the sunlight. It was a warm summer day, mid-July. Dane and

Tincher and Diego were already mounted and waiting. Town beckoned. Spring roundup was over, and the stores and honky-tonks would be alive with men who had come in off the range for a few days. Atkins didn't like to keep anybody waiting, so he swung into the saddle, adjusted his reins, pulled his hat down, and touched his spurs to the dun horse. It stepped out right away, and the other riders put their mounts into motion as well.

The sun felt warm on his back, and the heat reflected up from the dry ground. The smell of dust mixed with the aroma of sagebrush and the odor of horse, a familiar mixture. Everything seemed normal. Horse hooves thudded on the dry ground, saddles creaked, and the faint jingle of spurs carried on the summer air.

When the group arrived in town, Dane told the others they could go as they pleased. He said he wanted to check on an order in Chapman's Mercantile, and of course anyone who wanted to go into the store was welcome to do that as well.

Atkins decided he would go with Dane, as the sun was still high and he didn't care to start drinking any earlier than he had to. He imagined that at some point or another, it might be just as well if one of their group didn't get payday drunk.

The bell tinkled as Atkins walked into the store ahead of Dane. The interior was dim in contrast to the bright day outside, so Atkins paused to let his eyes adjust. The center aisle was empty all the way back to the counter, where the deer antlers hung on the wall. As Atkins stepped forward he heard the tread of feet on the wooden floor, and Chapman stepped out into the center aisle.

"Good afternoon, gentlemen," he said.

Atkins and Dane both returned the greeting.

Chapman rubbed his hands together. "What can I help you with today?"

Dane cleared his throat. "I thought we might check on a couple of things."

"Oh, uh-huh." Chapman turned and led the way back to the counter, his breadth blocking out the view of most of the aisle. "What might that be?" he asked, over his shoulder.

"The bathtub we spoke of a couple of months ago. You said you might have it in by now."

Chapman came to a stop in front of the counter, turned on his left foot, and faced the two men. He focused his clear, brown eyes on Dane. "Oh, yes. And which one was it we spoke about?"

Dane's voice carried a tone of impatience as he answered. "It was oblong, with a high back. I pointed it out to you in the catalog. I told you Hal wanted to get something like that for Laurel."

Chapman's head went up and then down. "Ah, yes. I remember." Then, leveling his gaze at Dane once again, he said, "I couldn't get it."

Dane's quick response sounded cross. "Do you mean that you ordered it and they wouldn't ship it?"

Chapman gave him a matter-of-fact look as if to imply that Dane was prying into the way he conducted his business. "I don't see where the details matter. If I couldn't get it, I couldn't get it."

Atkins saw Dane's chest go up and down as the young man's jaws tightened. It hadn't taken much to make him flare up.

Chapman spoke again. "Don't think I didn't try. Naturally I want to bring in merchandise I can sell. That's my business."

"A damn poor one, it seems."

Now Chapman had an edge in his voice, too. "I'm sure you could run it better yourself, but you've got your business and I've got mine."

"I suppose," said Dane. He lowered his head a little and gave Chapman a stern, upward look. "You make a fellow wonder if he should take his business elsewhere."

Chapman had regained his matter-of-fact composure. "That would be your choice." Then, as if he had just finished measuring out an order of beans, he said, "And what was the other item you had in mind?"

Dane blinked and said, "Nothing. That was all."

Atkins imagined Dane had planned to ask about the hinges he had ordered for the door that led from the stable to the toolshed. Now it seemed as if Dane either didn't want to buy any more goods from Chapman than he had to, or he didn't want to give Chapman the opportunity of turning him down again.

Dane looked at Atkins and motioned with his chin.

Atkins nodded, and Dane turned and headed for the door.

In the suspended instant in which Atkins turned to fall in behind Dane, his vacant gaze took in a figure and a face. It was Mrs. Chapman, standing in the dim recess of the store beyond where Dane had stood. She had a look on her face, a look that said she had tried to catch Dane's attention and had failed. It was an expression that, as she then transferred it to Atkins, became a conveyance of recognition. It acknowledged that he knew something.

Atkins was now walking toward the door, his boot heels sounding on the floor behind Dane's. The clomp and jingle seemed to fill the air as Atkins's thoughts caught up with what he had just seen.

Mrs. Chapman's look said that he knew something; it said he knew she had reason to look at him that way; it said he knew she looked at him because she had missed catching Dane's eye.

There was a degree of confidence that he recognized, as if they had known each other well. Her look had said he could be trusted. He understood all of this before he had taken three steps, so that in the instant when he knew he should have done something else, it was too late. He couldn't change course now, even as he intuited that the role of go-between had settled on him and that he should have contrived to cross paths with Mrs. Chapman.

He would have to come back, he thought. He would have to try again, because it was too late to try now. He would have to do it in some way by which he could sidestep the bean merchant. Not wanting to give away anything now, he did not look back, not even when he got to the door and could have glanced back as a matter of course. He doubted that he would have seen Mrs. Chapman anyway, and he was confident she knew he had caught her look.

Out on the sidewalk, as the doorbell tinkled behind them, Dane spoke in a lowered voice. "What a son of a bitch. He just didn't want to, that was all."

"To hell with him," said Atkins.

Dane sniffed. "I guess so." He looked up and down the street. "I guess we might as well find us a barrelhouse."

Atkins nodded. "I think Tincher and Diego

went to the Horseshoe. That's where the horses are."

"Well, let's go there, then."

The two of them turned to their left and walked down the sidewalk. They came to the corner, continued on their side of the street for another block, and then crossed the main street catercorner to arrive at the Horseshoe.

As they walked into the saloon, the sunny world outside gave way to the shadowy, smoky atmosphere of men milling and talking. Atkins heard the slap of a leather dice cup on top of the bar and the scraping sound of a chair being pushed away from a table.

He looked down the bar and saw Diego standing with one foot on the rail and looking straight ahead at nothing more significant than a troop of whiskey bottles. Beyond Diego, to the young man's left, Tincher stood half-turned, in conversation with another man. The conversation was apparently ending, as Tincher turned back to face the bar. The other man moved away, with his back to Tincher and anyone who might have just walked in. Atkins did not need to see his face, though, to know who it was. The flat-crowned, broad-brimmed, charcoal-colored hat belonged to no one but Fey.

Atkins and Dane stood by the bar on Diego's right. Dane called for drinks for the four of them and then gave a look around the bar. Without settling his gaze on anything in particular, he brought his attention back to the bar, where a glass of whiskey now stood in front of him. As he picked up his drink, he cocked his right eyebrow and looked sideways at Atkins.

"The son of a bitch is downright cheeky, isn't he?"

Atkins shrugged. "That and then some." He laid his hand to rest on his drink. "To hell with him."

Atkins stalled with his drink as Dane drank his and called for another. On the other side of the sullen boss of the NB, Diego stood without speaking. Beyond him, Tincher had fallen into an animated conversation with another cowpuncher, a fellow with bulging eyes and a large bushy mustache. Atkins felt a general uneasiness, despite the tranquilizing atmosphere of smoke, liquor fumes, and muffled conversation. He thought back to the suspended moment in which he had caught Mrs. Chapman's glance, and he knew he should go back to the store. But he didn't have a clear idea of how to go about it.

He toyed with his drink a little longer, taking small sips, until he decided he would just walk past the store and see if an idea came to him.

He tossed off the last of his drink and set the glass on the bar. "I think I'll go water the horses," he said. "I'll be back in a little while."

Dane and Diego both nodded, and Tincher

showed no awareness of having heard him.

Back out in the bright sunlight, Atkins cast a glance in the direction of the store, then cut straight across the street. Before he reached the sidewalk, he decided to walk in the street itself, so he veered left and walked toward the horses.

When he got to the dun horse, he fiddled with the front cinch for a moment, hoping he would sense the best way of crossing paths with Mrs. Chapman. He kept an eye on the front door of the mercantile, but he saw no movement. Then two men in range riding clothes came down the sidewalk toward him and went into the store.

Atkins waited for about as long as he thought it would take for Chapman to get his hooks into the two customers, and then he stepped up onto the sidewalk. He moved toward the door, uncertain, until without a tinkling of the bell the door opened.

It was as if it had all been planned ahead of time—the woman emerging from the store, a rustle of garments, her hand moving toward his, the envelope in his hand and then his vest pocket, and the retreating figure of the woman as she disappeared through the still-open doorway.

Atkins stood for a few seconds in the bright daylight, then stepped down into the street again and untied the horses. He did not have a sense of anyone having seen the exchange, but he did not look around, either. As he led the horses out into the middle of the wide street, he imagined that even if someone had happened to be looking, it would have been hard to see anything definite.

Back in the Horseshoe, things hadn't changed much. Dane and the two hired hands stood in the same places. Tincher was talking to the bartender and making broad, waving motions with his left hand. Dane glanced at Tincher and then at Atkins.

"Back, huh? You weren't gone long."

"I didn't have much to do." It occurred to Atkins that Dane might have thought he had gone off to a pleasure parlor.

Dane gave a light nod and said, "Oh." Dane motioned for the bartender to serve Atkins another drink.

Atkins waited until the bartender poured the drink and went back to stand in front of Tincher. Then he took the folded envelope out of his right pocket, transferred it to his left hand, and held it up almost to the level of the bar.

Dane looked down, looked up at Atkins, and then took the letter that was offered to him. He slipped it inside his shirt. "Thanks," he said.

"Don't mention it."

Dane raised his eyebrows. "I think I have a pretty good idea of what it says."

"Uh-huh."

"I think someone put the kibosh on someone else's comin' and goin'."

Atkins nodded. "Seems like it. Things look like they're nailed down pretty tight."

Dane screwed his mouth around to the left, then relaxed it. "It figures. When you were gone, Tincher told me he heard Chapman had sold that bathtub to someone else."

"Really?"

"Uh-huh. He says it went out to the Argentine Ranch."

A thought flickered. "He must have heard it from Fey."

"I'd imagine."

Atkins drew his brows together. "Had he already heard that before you told him anything?"

"Well, I think he knew that was what we were goin' to check on, but when he asked me how things were in the mercantile, I told him. Then he told me what he had heard."

Atkins shook his head. "Seems like some people know more than they should."

"Could be," Dane said, "but I don't think it matters much." He took a drink of whiskey. "I think I'll go out back for a minute."

Atkins looked at his drink and then at the other two NB men. Tincher was still talking and waving his hand, and Diego seemed to be following the conversation. From what Atkins overheard, he gathered that Tincher had worked on a railroad crew at one time and had helped build bridges. The bartender, who showed a capacity to absorb any number of long stories, gave a heavy-lidded nod every half minute or so.

Dane came back and took his place at the bar, blocking out part of Tincher's monologue. "Just about what I thought," he said, giving a down-turned expression.

Atkins met his gaze. "Uh-huh. Well, like you say, it all adds up."

Dane's face tightened. "And like you said, to hell with him." He picked up his drink and looked at it, then squinted as a bitter smile appeared on his face.

The saloon resumed its dull tone. Dane sulked and Tincher talked on. The drift of the conversation had come around to women, as it often did with Tincher. He was telling how the women worked in tents when they followed the railroad camps. His voice was louder now.

"Never anything to worry about, though. There's always women."

Diego's voice cut in. "Yeah, but they always cost a lot of money."

Tincher lifted his drink and took a sip, as if to heighten the drama of his response. "They cost less that way than the other way." He tilted his head back a little and looked down at Diego. "You now, they've got a sayin' when a fella has himself a little girlfriend and she does everything so sweet he wants to marry her. They say, why buy the cow if you get the milk for free? Well, that doesn't work so well out here, 'cause there's damn few women. So most of the time you have to buy the milk, but it's still cheaper than buyin' the whole cow."

"Is that right?" said Dane.

"That's right. You take a fella that's married, and it'll cost him everything he makes for the rest of his life. A workin' man can't afford to get married. But he can always afford a woman, if he don't spend his wages too soon."

Atkins saw the familiar smile, the gap-toothed leer, that often went with Tincher's lewd talk.

Dane was looking at Tincher but said nothing.

Tincher, with an audience of four now, including the bartender, was warming to his subject. "Yessir, that's the way to go. Don't worry about any of 'em thataway. One's as good as another. Black or white, blond or brunette, they've all got the same gadget. And I've never worried about any in particular."

"Sounds like you've done just fine," said Dane, his voice dry.

Tincher gave his smile. "Seen a little bit of it." Then he added, "Blond and brunette both."

Atkins felt Dane getting tense. Playing in to Tincher's line of talk was a sign of impatience on Dane's part. He sometimes found ways of stifling the subject, but he didn't say anything in response this time. Atkins thought some of Tincher's remarks might have been deliberate barbs; whether they were or not, they seemed to have carried some sting.

Atkins took a look at Tincher. It was hard to tell how deep the man was. He could aggravate others so well without trying that a fellow didn't know how much credit to give him for being subtle. It was possible that he knew something about Mrs. Chapman, and it was possible that he had detected some of Dane's suppressed interest in Laurel, but even at that, it was hard to see a purpose in putting a burr under the boss's blanket.

Atkins looked at his drink and then took a sip. The conversation had subsided for the moment, so the level of irritation had gone down. Atkins wondered how long the NB crew would stay in the Horseshoe. For his own part, he didn't have any plans beyond the drink he was fidgeting with, and he didn't have the impression that Dane or anyone else had thoughts any more advanced than his. The atmosphere of the saloon had gone sluggish, or at least it seemed that way to Atkins. He had a sense of inertia pervading the place, as if time had slowed down because no one had the initiative to wind the clock.

Out of the milling of the crowd there emerged a drab, broad-brimmed hat, a flat-crowned object the color of burned-out firewood. Even before he saw the straight hair and the lean face, Atkins knew who it was.

Fey's eyes moved from Tincher to Dane. If he had taken in Diego or Atkins, he didn't show it. The brown eyes settled on Dane, who had rolled and lit a cigarette.

"Mr. Norden."

"Yessir." Dane tapped his cigarette to let the ash drop to the floor, then put the cigarette back to his lips and left it there.

"No need to call me sir. I'm a hired man."

"Uh-huh." Dane looked at Fey as if he was trying to read an answer to some question—maybe the question of why Fey was taking the trouble to say hello. Dane nodded. "I remember you well enough. You work for the Argentine Ranch."

Fey showed his teeth. "I sure do."

Without touching it, Dane rolled the cigarette from the left side of his mouth to the right. "Uh-huh. I trust that you had a good roundup."

Fey tipped his head back. "In what way?"

Dane spit a fleck of tobacco out the left corner of his mouth. "In your calf crop." He did not say "of course," but it was in his tone. If spring roundup was for branding new calves, there was one main way in which things could go well.

Atkins found himself trying to place Fey. He wondered why the man would go out of his way to make conversation with someone he wasn't that familiar with. Atkins shook his head. Fey was like a word written in another language—clear in outline but vacant in meaning.

"It was good enough." Fey had his thumbs hooked on his belt. He was not wearing a gun, but the gesture seemed to be a habitual one to draw attention in that area. "And yourselves?" he asked. "Did you have a lot of twin calves?"

Atkins caught a spark of hostility in the air as Dane answered.

"Not at all. I'd say our cow-to-calf ratio is less than five to four."

Fey showed his teeth again. "Well, that's probably as good as anyone is doin'."

Dane showed his own teeth in a smile that might have been a mimic. "Seems just about right to us. And as far as that goes, there was a rep from another outfit present at every calf we branded."

Fey made an artificial frown. "I wouldn't have thought otherwise."

"Then why did you mention it?"

"Just makin' conversation." Fey's voice was calm.

Dane took a drag on his cigarette. "Well, I guess it was neighborly," he said, flicking his ash and not looking at Fey.

"It's the way I like to be."

"Uh-huh."

The conversation hit a lull for a moment, and

Atkins thought Fey might leave it at that and move on. But the hope faded as the steady voice came back.

"Yessir, it's the way I like to be. Neighborly."

Dane glanced up at him but said nothing.

"I like to be sociable," said Fey, his voice pushing a little now.

"I see."

"Uh-huh. Especially when it looks like a friend and neighbor could use some company."

Dane gave him a questioning look. "What makes you say that?"

Fey showed his teeth. "Well, looks to me like you're hard up for company."

Dane took a last pull on his cigarette, dropped the stub on the floor, and ground it out with his boot heel. Then he shook his head and said, "I don't know what you're gettin' at."

"Oh, nothin' personal," said Fey. After a pause he added, "But it's plain as day."

"I didn't know that," said Dane, in a measured tone.

Atkins was sure Dane knew he was being baited, but it was also apparent that Fey knew how to poke here and poke there until he opened a hole.

"Sure it is," Fey went on. "Look at what you've got for company. You've got a sheepherder masqueradin' as a horse wrangler, and

90

your grandpa masqueradin' as a chuck wagon cook."

"Their company is good enough for me."

"No doubt," retorted Fey, "but it's plain that you miss someone."

Atkins felt a chill creep up and across his neck and shoulders. Fey seemed to have made some deliberate effort to find out where Dane's sore spots were.

Dane was doing all right at keeping a cool head. "Is that right?" he asked.

Fey smiled. "Yeah, it is. Havin' to guess, I'd say it's your little brother."

"What about him?" was the quick reply.

Atkins shook his head. He couldn't follow what Fey was leading to. A minute earlier, it seemed as if Fey was prodding Dane about his foundered love affair, and now he was off on another angle.

"Oh, nothin'," answered Fey.

Dane's hand moved toward his drink and then stopped. "If you've got somethin' to say, you could leave him out of it."

Fey took a moment to answer. "Maybe I was wrong."

Dane looked at him.

"How would I know, really?" Then, after a pause, Fey said, "I don't take you for a mooner like the little leppy. It just seems like you're missing someone, and I don't know who it could be, unless it was someone from your family."

Atkins felt the chill again. He was sure some of this had come by way of Tincher, but he couldn't figure out what part.

Dane shook his head in a firm, tight motion. "I don't think you need to—"

Fey's voice cut in. "Just a guess, knowin' how close you all are." Then, before Dane could answer, he added, "I heard you all slept in the same bed."

Dane's flat-open right hand came up and around and made a resounding smack on Fey's cheek. "That's enough of that. Say anything you want about me, and I'll answer to it. But you leave decent men and women out of it."

Fey had a smirk on his face. "Seems like you get hot pretty easy. You'd better watch yourself."

"I'd say the same for you. If you want to go at it, just say so."

"Thanks for the invitation," said Fey, "but I'd rather just leave you with a warnin'. Watch your back from now on."

Dane's expression was hard. "Try me face-to-face. Unless the only way you can do it is by back-shootin', you'll have about as much of a chance as a one-legged Indian at an ass-kickin' contest."

Fey made a thin smile. "That's cute. But I wasn't makin' a threat. It was neighborly advice. Don't think I'm the only one you ever offended."

"I wouldn't make that mistake," Dane said.

Chapter Six

Atkins held the triangle at chest height and rang the dinner bell by clanging the iron bar around the inside. As the clear notes ended on the summer air, he stilled the vibrations of the two instruments and turned back into the bunkhouse. He went to the nail on the wall and hung the triangle and bar, each with its leather thong.

Midsummer should be a more cheerful time, he thought as he went back to the kitchen. There were new calves growing on the range, and the grass had stayed green well into the summer. The Norden boys were putting up hay, fencing in the haystacks, and making plans to put in more corrals. They were building a ranch.

Although the incident with Fey was never mentioned out loud and the Argentine Ranch was referred to only in the most oblique ways, Frank Cobarde's outfit cast a feeling of gloom on the NB. So it seemed to Atkins, at least. He was sure everyone at the NB recognized that Fey's aggression was deliberate and that he was carrying out orders. The appropriation of the bathtub was less overt, but it still sized up as a provocation. Although it was a petty incident, it showed that Cobarde was willing to antagonize the Norden boys from more than one angle. It also showed that the boss of the Argentine Ranch had put out feelers and had engaged at least one ally.

As nearly as Atkins could tell, it was not a personal issue. Cobarde had very little acquaintance with the Norden brothers, but from all appearances he coveted their land and resented their determination to keep it. It was no matter if it meant something to them or to any family they might build; he wanted it, and he was willing to push them off.

Atkins was sure that the threat of trouble loomed in the west. He doubted it would take the shape of a legion of dark riders coming in to run off the Norden brothers and their hired hands. Rather, he expected more gestures like the one he had seen, more encounters that carried menacing undertones.

The atmosphere of the kitchen softened his thoughts. The aroma of fresh coffee, blended with the smell of bacon grease and fried beef, hung rich in the air. Atkins raised his eyebrows and smiled. To hell with the Argentine Ranch for the moment. There was good grub to be eaten. Touching the handle of the iron skillet nearest him and finding it hot, he used a cloth pot holder to steady the pan as he forked out the fried steaks. He set the skillet aside and scooted the other one close, then lifted the hot, juicy steaks and stacked them on the platter with the first batch.

.The men came trooping into the bunkhouse as Atkins set the platter of steaks on the table. Then he went to the kitchen for the pot of beans. Uncovering the iron pot, he caught a whiff of pork rind and beans. When it came to bunkhouse food, it didn't get much better—unless there was an apple pie, which he didn't have at the moment. He set the pot of beans on the table, then an enamel bowl of cold biscuits and a pot of hot coffee.

Tincher was the first one to arrive at the table. His hair was mashed down where his hat had been, and it was damp around the edges where he had washed his face. He had his head lifted a little, like a coyote sniffing the promise of a dead cow, and his loose smile was in tone with both his good eye and his bad one.

Behind him came Diego and Dane, also with clean faces and damp hair. Diego was buttoning his cuffs, while Dane was rolling up his sleeves.

Tincher put his hands to the bottom of his rib cage, as if assessing how much room he had. "Smells great," he said. "It looks like you outdone yourself again, Tom."

Atkins nodded. "I hope everyone likes it."

Tincher seemed never to miss a chance for a comment. "If someone doesn't, it's got to be his fault." He smiled, showing the gap beside the front left tooth.

Atkins stood waiting as the other three men sat down, Tincher on one side and the other two men across from him. It seemed as if something was missing, but he supposed it was just Hal, who would be sitting down at a smaller table with his pretty wife at the same moment. Atkins cast his glance up and down the table. Satisfied that everything was in order, he sat down at the end of the table closest to the kitchen.

Tincher loaded up his plate with beefsteak and beans, and as usual he salted his food before tasting it. Diego served himself a full plate, also, then paused for a moment as he usually did. Atkins assumed Diego said grace to himself at such a time, and it seemed as if the other men had formed the same impression. Although it did not stop them from serving food or digging in, they seemed to have arrived at an understanding that for at least those few seconds, no one spoke.

When Diego picked up his fork, the truce was over.

Tincher, with his head lowered over his plate, paused between mouthfuls. "Dago, you'll have to tell the folks back home there's at least one white man can cook a pot of beans with the best of 'em. Don't you think?"

Diego looked at Atkins and smiled. "Tom always fixes good food. That's for sure."

Tincher sopped a biscuit in the bean juice. " 'Course, he makes beans a little different. These are swimmin' in juice, with little pieces of bacon or ham, it looks like. Whereas the Mexicans, they like to mash 'em into a paste."

Diego cut off a corner of steak. "Oh, they cook beans this way, too. They call 'em *frijoles charros.*"

"Is that right?" Tincher said without looking up.

"Uh-huh."

Atkins noticed Dane look up and then go back to his meal.

Tincher rotated his plate and cut into his steak. "I always wondered why they mashed the beans."

Diego shrugged. "It's easier to eat 'em with tortillas that way."

Tincher spoke around a mouthful of steak. "I guess I knew that."

The men ate without speaking for a long moment, until Tincher picked up his knife again. "The other thing I always figgered," he said, "is that beans must be good for puttin' lead in your pencil."

Diego glanced up but said nothing.

Tincher had a half-smile as he paused from cutting his steak. "You know what I mean, don't you?"

"Oh, yeah. You always like to talk about your *pito*."

"I'm not just talkin' about mine. What I mean is, I figger beans must put lead in your pencil because you see so much evidence, what with the way all the Mexicans breed like flies."

Atkins could tell Dane was getting tense as silence hung over the table.

Finally Diego spoke. "If that's what you say."

Tincher cut off another bite of steak. "It's not just what I say. It's what I've seen. Just one kid after another. Why, it's nothin' to have a dozen kids in a family."

Diego held his knife and fork in each hand, resting on the edge of the table. "So what? What's wrong with that?"

"Oh, nothin'. I've seen a lot of 'em I'd like to lift their skirt and put a watermelon under it, but I wonder if they don't get tired of spendin' their whole life knocked up and splay-footed."

Dane raised his head and gave Tincher a clear look of dislike.

Atkins recalled the way Dane had tightened up on earlier occasions when Tincher and then Fey made remarks that gigged him. He could feel Dane's patience was wearing thin again.

"That's up to them," said Diego.

"I suppose so." Tincher rose halfway from his chair and served himself some more beans. "You know, the other thing I've wondered is how they always get it done. With that many kids, and the little houses they live in, you wonder how they get a bed all to themselves, or whether it matters."

Now Dane spoke up. "You mean *you* wonder."

Tincher shrugged. "I guess anyone would."

Dane gave him a hard look. "Some people try not to worry so much about things like that."

"Well, I just thought—"

"What the hell is it to you, anyway?"

Tincher set down his knife and fork and gave Dane an insolent look with his one good eye widened. "I didn't know you were so touchy."

"You don't know much."

Tincher tipped his head to the right. "Maybe I don't. But I know what I've seen."

"What's that?"

Atkins felt that the conversation was slipping out of control, as if they were all on the verge of a dangerous moment as they waited for the answer.

The half-smile returned as Tincher's head straightened up and tipped back to the right.

"Like I said. Just a lot of evidence. Spraddle-legged women, and men that are always ready to slip it to 'em." Tincher turned his head to look at Diego and then back toward Atkins. "Sometimes that dark hair reminds you of the mane on a bay horse, and you wonder if they got a little of the animal in 'em."

"Is that why you wanna lift their skirt?" Diego asked. "To do it with an animal?"

Tincher showed the gap between his teeth. "Not so much, but it would give me a different look at a dark-haired woman."

Dane slapped his knife on the table with a suddenness that made Atkins think of Laurel. Tincher's earlier remark about who might sleep in the same bed had brought to mind the provoking slur by Fey, and Atkins imagined Tincher was trying to needle Dane in a similar way. Now the comment about a dark-haired woman seemed to have hit its mark.

Dane's voice was cold. "Just shut up, Mike."

Tincher made a frown.

"I mean it. Just shut up. I've had enough of your two-bit talk for today."

Tincher raised his eyebrows. "By God, you *are* touchy. That's bound to get you in trouble."

Dane pushed himself away from the table and stood up. "Not with the likes of you." Then he seemed to get a better grip on himself. He shook his head and said, "I've just had enough, Mike, and I don't want it to get any worse. I'll go make out your pay."

Tincher looked up with his good eye widened. "Probably be just as well."

Atkins glanced at Diego, and he imagined the young man was just as glad as he was that neither of them had to say a thing. For once, Tincher's push to get in the last word was tolerable.

That evening, when Tincher had packed his gear and ridden away, the atmosphere was more cheerful at the NB. Dane had a smile on his face as he rolled and lit his after-supper cigarette. He and Diego sat on opposite sides of the table now, and even though there were only three men who sat down to eat, Atkins did not feel that there was much missing.

The general mood got even better when Hal dropped in for a little visit. It came out in conversation that he was going to take Laurel to Cheyenne the next day to see a doctor. He was quick to add that it was nothing serious, just a little checkup for women things. He and Dane made up a list of items for him to buy while he was in Cheyenne. The two brothers seemed determined to do without Chapman's merchandise to whatever extent they could. On his list, Hal had a hundred pounds of beans, two hundred pounds of flour, a couple of slabs of bacon, a supply of canned goods, a bag of dried apples, and a pair of hinges. Atkins appreciated their working it down to that detail.

Hal and Laurel were gone two days, leaving early on one day and getting back late on the next day. They brought home a full supply of food items as well as some odds and ends of dry goods and hardware. On the following morning, Hal came for breakfast, as a way of letting Laurel get some rest after the trip. No one gave any sign of being in a hurry. When Atkins finished with the dishes, the two brothers and Diego were still sitting at the table beneath a haze of cigarette smoke.

Atkins stood for a moment at the end of the table and then sat down. He had the sense that Hal wanted to say something, which turned out to be the case.

Everything had gone fine on the trip to Cheyenne, he said. There was nothing to worry about with Laurel. The doctor said she was in tip-top shape, which was good, as she was in the family way.

Dane broke out in a wide smile, and Diego beamed. Hal glowed with what seemed like a mixture of embarrassment and pride, which was normal for a boyish young man who had to share that sort of news with other men.

"You want a boy or a girl?" asked Diego.

"Either one would make us happy, but naturally, I'd rather have a boy the first time."

Atkins smiled. "How about Laurel?"

"I think she wants a little boy, too, the first time." Hal looked at Dane with an expression of pure delight. "And she agrees that if it's a little boy, we'll call it Dane."

Dane's eyes got big. "You didn't tell her I told you that, did you?"

"Well, sort of. But I told her it was what I would like, and she thought it was fine."

Dane looked around at the others. "Now I'm the one that's embarrassed."

Atkins raised an eyebrow. "Good. I think Hal needed some help in that area." He looked at the proud father-to-be. "Congratulations, Hal. I hope everything goes well."

"Thanks, Tom. Everything looks fine, and we're as happy as we can be."

Dane shook his head. "I wish you hadn't told her it was my idea."

"Oh, don't worry. It doesn't matter who thought of it first. We both like the idea, so that's good enough."

The men finished their coffee and got up to go to work. Atkins, having tidied up the kitchen, decided to go out and lend a hand. Dane sent Diego to make a round in the horse pasture to check on things while he and Hal put hinges on the door that led from the stable to the toolroom. Atkins was glad to see that detail being tended to, as it opened a passageway that could be useful. Once the boys had gotten the door loose from being nailed shut, Atkins held it in place, balanced by a crowbar, as the boys screwed in the hinges.

"By the way," said Hal, holding pressure against the door as Dane drove the screws, "I think I got us another hired hand."

Dane paused in his work. "Oh, really?"

"Yep. Seemed like a good-natured fellow. Said he just got into town and needed a job."

"Is he any kind of a hand, or do you know?"

"He says he is. Of course, they all do. I told him to come by, and we'd try him out."

"Oh. Has he got somethin' keepin' him there in Cheyenne?"

"Nothing serious. I think he wanted to lay over, get a decent night's sleep, have himself a bath and a shave, and come on out here in his own good time."

"You expect him today?"

"Oh, I think so."

Dane pushed out his lower lip and nodded. "What's his name?"

"Porter. Charley Porter."

In the latter part of the morning, Atkins went back to the bunkhouse and kitchen, where he put together a midday meal. With Hal having gone back to his own cottage for dinner with Laurel, the table at the bunkhouse had only three seats

104

occupied once again, but the atmosphere was pleasant. Dane said that he and Hal were going to ride over to the north about ten miles, to see how their cattle were scattered out in that direction. He told Diego he could ride along, and Atkins understood that Diego was being invited to take the part of a regular cowpuncher for the afternoon.

After dinner, when the men had ridden out, Atkins cleaned up the dishes and put the kitchen in order. After that, he decided to lie down on his bunk for a short while. It was a quiet, peaceful afternoon, and he appreciated having a few minutes to himself. He had a reassuring sense of solitude, of being sequestered in a bunkhouse out on the vast plains with open country stretching in all directions. It was like being a pinpoint on a map, a speck on a large expanse with nothing near.

Then he recalled that Laurel was over in the other house, and he wondered if she appreciated the isolation as he did. He also wondered if she had a sense of his presence in the bunkhouse or if she had any awareness of him at all. He wouldn't expect her to, as she would probably be thinking of Hal. For his own part, though, Atkins allowed himself to think of her as a sort of kindred spirit, another person who tended the fire and the skillets while the others rode out to do what they considered the real work.

The sound of sharp thuds on the roof made Atkins realize he had drifted into a light sleep. Now he was awake. He recognized the sound that had brought him to consciousness. It wasn't just heavy raindrops; it was hail.

The drumming came thicker now, intensifying in just a minute or two, as hail did. It sounded like a crew of forty men hammering on the roof. Now the racket grew stronger, almost to a steady roar. Atkins sat up on his bunk but kept still, listening to the rattle and knowing that the best thing to do was stay away from windows and just wait out the storm. Hail usually didn't last long, but it could do a great deal of damage in a short while. No amount of worry would change the results, so a person just waited to see what the outcome would be.

After about ten minutes, the roar began to let up, and a few minutes later the storm had passed over. Atkins got up from his bunk and went to the door to look out.

The ranch yard outside was covered in a blanket of marble-sized hailstones, and the buildings had water running off the eaves. The air smelled fresh and alive, and it felt charged with energy. Calm prevailed in the aftermath of the storm, but it could have done quite a bit of damage if the stones had been much larger. Even small hail could damage broad-leafed plants, and it could sting a person. Atkins knew that much from having been caught out in the open in a hail-storm.

The door to the little house opened, and Laurel appeared in the doorway. Atkins waved, and she waved back. He decided to walk over to within speaking distance. He put on his hat and walked out onto the carpet of crunchy hailstones.

"Are you all right?" he called out.

"Yes," she answered. "It gave me a little fright, but it didn't hurt anything. I *am* worried about the boys, though."

Atkins looked toward the north. "It's hard to tell if they got any hail out that way, or if they did, if it was any worse."

She looked in the same direction. "I'd like to walk out and take a look if we could."

Atkins glanced at the sky. It was still overcast, but the dark, heavy clouds were moving east. "I think we should be all right."

She went back into the house and then came out wearing a gray wool coat. She did not wear a hat or scarf, though, and her dark hair cascaded over the collar of her coat. She had a worried look on her face, but otherwise she looked fresh and hopeful, as a young wife might. Atkins felt like a protective uncle as she fell in beside him.

As they walked out toward the low hills north of the ranch, Atkins noticed that the hail was melting in the open areas. Where it had collected at the base of sagebrush and yucca, it was still intact, in little mounds of ice. As Atkins and Laurel climbed the nearest hill, he saw that the cedar trees also sheltered small accumulations of hail. Little sprigs from the trees lay about, and the fresh smell of cedar, released by the cuts and breaks in the foliage, hovered sweet on the air. He was struck by the contrast between the pretty smell, which seemed benevolent, and the indiscriminate force of the storm.

They reached the top of the hill, where they had a good view of the plains to the north. Everything looked calm. No menacing clouds lay in that direction, but in the east the skies were dark. Atkins knew that hailstorms often cut a path, wreaking devastation in one spot but doing no harm at all a half-mile away.

"Doesn't look like it did much out north," he said. "But it's hard to tell."

Laurel nodded, still gazing in the direction where Hal would be. "I just know it can get fierce, though."

"Well, it can. But let's try not to worry. They'll be riding in before long, anyway, and we'll find out then."

She looked at him, and a trace of optimism returned to her face as she smiled. Then, after glancing again at the empty plain, she turned and started walking down the hill.

Back at the yard, after thanking Atkins, she turned and went into the little house. Atkins looked at the sky, which was clearing out to an innocent shade of blue, and then went back into the bunkhouse.

Later that afternoon, the three riders came in from the range. Atkins heard the hoofbeats, soft on the damp ground, and went to the door. Dane was leading a horse with an empty saddle, and behind the first two horses rode Diego. Atkins wondered where Hal was until he heard voices and saw Hal going into the little house.

Atkins walked over toward the stable and got there as Dane swung down from the saddle. Atkins asked how the weather had been, and Dane said they had gotten a little rain and nothing more. Atkins told him about the hailstorm and said it didn't look as if there was any serious damage.

Dane looked around the ranch yard and nodded.

"Probably one more time to be glad you're not a wheat farmer," Atkins said.

Dane smiled. "That's right. If we go broke, it won't be from getting hailed out." He motioned with his head. "Was Laurel scared?"

Atkins shrugged. "About normal, I guess."

Dane yawned as he pulled loose the back cinch on his horse. "Well, she's got Hal to take care of her, so everything should be all right."

Atkins went back into the bunkhouse and started getting supper ready. A little while later, along about evening, he heard voices out front. One of the voices sounded unfamiliar, so he opened the door and stepped out to take a look. In the middle of the yard, between the bunkhouse and the stable, stood Dane and another man about the same age. The newcomer, a fellow of average height and build, had a relaxed air about him. He wore a hat with a short, round brim and a bandanna hatband. The hat was tipped back on his head, and his brown hair lay on his forehead down to his eyebrows. He wore a brown vest, unbuttoned, over a gray cotton work shirt. Standing with his thumbs hooked in his belt, he had a set of reins in his right hand. Behind his right elbow, in a placid stance, stood a dappled gray horse with a bedroll tied to the back of the saddle.

The young man glanced his way, and Atkins nodded. Dane half-turned and, seeing Atkins, waved for him to come over.

"Tom, this is Charley Porter. He's the new hand that Hal told us about. He'll be one of the bunch."

Charley had friendly blue eyes and a cheerful expression on his face. As Atkins shook hands with him, he took a liking to the young man. It was quite an improvement on Tincher, he thought.

"Welcome to the place," said Atkins.

Charley smiled. "Thanks. When I get welcomed by the cook, I know I'm off to a good start." He glanced at Dane. " 'Course, gettin' here after the day's work is done is pretty slick, too."

Dane laughed. "That, and showin' up in time for the supper bell. I'd say that's a good start. Not to mention gettin' here after the hailstorm has passed over."

Charley got his horse put away and his gear stowed in the bunkhouse in time for supper. He sat down at the table next to Diego, across from Dane. With his easy manner, he was already on friendly terms with Dane and Hal, and he was quick to make friends with the other hired hand. Before supper was over, it was evident that he knew how to pronounce Diego's name. It also seemed to Atkins that Diego liked to pronounce Charley's name, with a little lilt to the "r" and a clipped last syllable. It became evident that Charley would fit in well. He didn't make insinuating comments, nor did he have the irritating habit of always having something to say. Remembering the undercurrent that always ran through the conversations that Tincher promoted, Atkins appreciated the change.

Over the course of the next few days, another characteristic of Charley's became evident. He liked to whistle and sing. Atkins would hear him out in the yard whistling, and sometimes he would sing a verse or two of a song as he was

111

cleaning up or walking through the bunkhouse. In the evening, between supper and bedtime, when he and Diego were resting on their bunks, the two of them would take turns listening to each other's songs.

Diego sang in Spanish, soft songs that Atkins did not understand even when he was reclined close by on his own bunk. The few words he knew in Spanish were not enough to give him a sense of actual meaning, but he could tell that most of Diego's songs were about sadness and lost love.

Charley knew the sad songs, too, such as "Lorena" and "Bury Me Not on the Lone Prairie," but he also knew the lively ones like "Sweet Betsy from Pike" and "My Lulu Gal." For every song he knew about death and tragic love, he knew another about petticoats. A song might vary from one singer to another, or a verse from one song might show up in another, but most songs a fellow heard in a bunkhouse or around a campfire were familiar. Most of Charley's songs were that way, but one evening he sang a song that Atkins had never heard even a part of before. This time Charley sat up on the edge of his bunk, and with his eyes shining, he sang the verses:

"Put your cute foot in the stirrup
And come take a ride with me,
We will ride the trail together
'Neath the sun and sky so free.

For the Norden Boys

"And then when the ride is over,
    Put your horse in my corral,
Put your gentle hand in mine and
    Tell me you will be my gal.

"Hand in hand, the best of partners,
    Side by side in harmony—
For the wind has whispered to us
    That our love is destiny.

"Put your arms around me, darlin',
    Put your tender lips to mine;
Put your head upon my shoulder
    As we let our souls entwine.

"Let me hold you close forever
    In a golden reverie—
May I always earn the honor
    That you put your trust in me."

Atkins wondered if Charley had composed the song himself or if he had heard it from someone else. Either way, he sang the song as if it were his. There was a way a singer had of taking a song into his own heart. A fellow who knew a great number of songs would sing many of them just for fun, for the singing, but now and then he would sing one that carried more emotion. Atkins, who considered himself less than an average singer, still knew the feeling. It was as if a song spoke to a fellow, and then, when he took

113

it in and it became a part of him, it spoke for him. That was the way he felt it was with Charley with this song.

"I don't believe I've heard that song before," Atkins said.

Charley twisted his mouth to one side. "No, I don't think it's got around very much."

"Sometimes you wonder where a song comes from."

"Oh, some of 'em come from a dozen different places and never sound the same way twice. Others, they come from a good horse or a pretty girl."

"That would be my guess on the one you just sang."

Charley seemed to be making a point of studying the fingernails on his left hand. "Yep. I'd guess the same. There's probably a pretty girl somewhere behind that song."

And so a little cheer came into the bunkhouse at the NB. Atkins didn't miss Tincher at all, but sometimes he thought about the man. He wondered how much of a danger the former NB hand might be. Atkins was sure Tincher had gone out of his way to irritate Dane, and if he wasn't already in league with Fey, it would be easy for him to find favor at the Argentine Ranch. Atkins doubted that he and the boys had seen the last of the leering cowpuncher, but whatever might come, he was glad Tincher was gone.

Chapter Seven

Atkins swung the mattock and sank the blade into the dry ground, then with a wrench of the handle pried loose a chunk of earth. He raised the mattock and brought it down again, pleased with the force he was able to get out of the thick-bladed, heavy-shanked tool. He pulled and loosened another section of earth. Repeating the stroke a dozen times, and adjusting his feet each time for just the right reach, he soon had his fire pit laid out. Then he traded the mattock for the shovel and dug out the loose dirt, mounding it all around the edge of the hole.

He liked to surround a fire pit with rocks, but he had not seen any stones handy out here on this spot on the plains. From where he stood he could not see any trees, either—just dirt and grass and cactus—but he did have a pile of fire-wood in the wagon. With a little management, he should have enough wood until they moved to the next camp.

Digging the pit and building the fire were jobs that often fell to the horse wrangler, but Diego was off grazing the herd, and Atkins didn't mind doing the menial work. He knew he might not have as much strength in his arms and legs as he once did, and he was glad to keep as fit as he could. He liked the feeling of warmth spreading through his muscles; it made him feel capable.

Atkins looked at the sky and then at his stack of firewood, figuring the time he would need to cook the noon meal. He had three kinds of wood—sagebrush, cedar, and some nondescript deadfall. He decided to use some of the junk wood first, as he had the most of it and he imagined it would burn the fastest. He laid a fire and got it burning, then cut up a chunk of beef shoulder as the flames burned down. After setting up the tripod and getting a Dutch oven hanging on the chain, he daubed a couple of spoonfuls of bacon grease into the pot. The rich oily smell rose up on the warm air as the gobs melted. Then Atkins dumped in the meat, which sputtered in the hot grease.

This part of the shoulder meat, being a bit tough, would cook well if it simmered in a gravy for at least an hour. Atkins savored the smell of searing meat as he mixed the water and flour for the gravy. He turned the meat, added salt and pepper, and waited a few more minutes before pouring in the flour and water. Stirring the mixture every minute or so, he watched it turn brown and begin to bubble. Then he put the lid on the Dutch oven and turned his attention to the rest of the camp.

The days were shorter now in late October, warm at midday but cool in the morning and evening. A fellow didn't need to look for shade. Instead, he enjoyed the strongest part of the day and tried to soak in the warmth. Come evening, he would hunch into a coat, and at bedtime he would be glad to have a canvas wrapped around the bedroll.

Fall roundup hadn't taken long, and the boys hadn't shipped many steers. Dane was sure they had come up short, so now they were out hunting strays, to get an idea of what they might have missed. In three days they had turned up fewer than a dozen head of their own cattle, with only a couple of steers that they would have shipped. The plan was to stay at it for a couple of more days, and then they would call it good for the season. Diego and Charley would be free to go; Atkins and Dane would settle in for another winter in the bunkhouse, while Hal and Laurel would do the same in their house.

Atkins set out the eating utensils. Dinner was

still an hour away, and he didn't have much to do. He had cold biscuits to go with the meat and gravy, so all he had left to do was fix a pot of coffee. After he had the coffeepot ready, he stood on the sunny side of the chuck wagon and looked out across the country.

Tawny grassland stretched away in all directions. The spot where he had chosen to set camp was just a speck in a sea of grass. Nothing began or ended here, or anywhere near. Tomorrow morning he would take the mattock and scrape the ridge of dirt back into the fire pit. He would pack up the camp and roll out, and the site would be just another spot with a few visible traces to tell that someone had been there.

Off to the west, several miles in the distance, the mountains rose above the plain. He could make out Silver Mountain among them. To the south, the low line of hills ran east toward the NB headquarters, which were vacant at the moment. Back around to the east, and a little farther south, lay the town of Farris, where Laurel was staying with her sister. From where he stood, Atkins could not see the Argentine Ranch, the NB buildings, the town, or any other object made by man. He knew that those places and others were out on the landscape, ensconced in the dips and rises of the country, but on the basis of what he could see, it looked like a vast tableland that men and animals roamed across in slow, random movements.

Atkins turned around and looked at the wagon, trying to think of some chore that would help pass the time until dinner. In a camp like this, far from wood and water, he didn't have much busy work. And with a small crew out on a short excursion, he didn't have to do much to put together a meal.

He picked up the knife he had used to cut the shoulder meat. Feeling the edge, he decided he could sharpen knives for a while. He dug out the whetstone from its cubbyhole in the chuck box, and after glancing around at the empty country, he turned his attention to sharpening knives.

When he finished with the butcher knife and the smaller paring knife, he lifted the lid on the Dutch oven and stirred the meat and gravy. The mess was coming along well enough. He settled the lid back in place and went to stand by the wagon again. He yawned. As a general rule it wasn't that hard to keep busy in a camp. He looked around the area just beyond the campsite, and it was all the same, just dirt and grass and cactus. He yawned again. Then he decided he would walk in widening circles around the camp until he found a rock.

It was a simple idea, but it gave him something definite to do. If he finished, he could look for another rock. If he didn't find one at all by the time the riders came in, at least he would be working with a purpose. And so he walked, looking up from the ground now and again to check on the surrounding landscape. Nothing changed from one glance to the next, regardless of whether he looked to the north, to the south, to the east, or to the west. Then he found a rock.

It was a medium-sized rock, about as big as a small loaf of bread he might bake in his Dutch oven. He dislodged it with the heel of his boot, then picked it up and carried it back to the camp. He set the rock against the ridge of dirt that lay on the lip of the fire pit. Checking the pot, he stirred the meat and gravy. Then he looked at the rock again. It would be an insignificant detail to a casual observer, but to Atkins it represented the difference between doing nothing and doing something. He tapped at it with the sole of his boot. It was good enough, as rocks went.

After putting a little more wood on the fire, Atkins looked over the plates and cups and silverware he had laid out. He went through his list of boarders—Diego, Charley, Hal, and Dane. They would be riding in before long, one at a time. When Charley was done he would go spell Diego, and when Diego had eaten he would go back to the horse herd. For as much as it was all rather uncomplicated, something nagged at the edge of Atkins's thoughts. Here they were, the NB crew, going out for a second look after the roundup was over, and they didn't seem to be gaining anything. Maybe all they were doing was confirming Dane's suspicion that they had lost some cattle. But even if they had, it was hard to do much about it if the cattle were gone. Atkins shook his head. Maybe it was good enough just to know that something was out of order.

Dane came riding in first. He brought the horse in on a slow walk, dismounted a few yards from the wagon, and led the animal to the front wheel, where he tied the reins.

"No one else in yet?"

Atkins shook his head.

Dane nodded and looked at the pot. "How long till chuck?"

"Oh, any time." Atkins set out the bowl of biscuits, then used his pothook to lift the lid off the Dutch oven.

Dane raised his eyebrows. "Smells like grub."

Atkins smiled and lifted his head. "That it does." Holding the pothook straight up in front of him, he lifted the pot off the chain and set it on the tailgate. "Dig in," he said. Then he set the coffeepot on the hook that hung on the chain. The firewood he had thrown on a little while earlier had burned down, and the coffeepot nestled in a good bed of coals.

Charley came riding in next and tied his horse to the other front wheel. He served himself a plate of grub and sat on the ground near Dane,

121

who listened to the rider's report about what he had seen.

Atkins did not serve himself anything yet. He stood by the fire pit, gazing at the orange coals and then looking up and around at the grassland every few minutes. When Hal came in, he would eat.

Dane's voice rose on the air. "I don't suppose anyone's been by here, Tom."

Atkins shook his head. "No, it's been pretty quiet."

Dane turned back to his plate and resumed eating.

A few minutes later, Hal came in. He tied his horse next to Dane's and walked straight to the tailgate, where he grabbed a plate and a spoon.

"Looks like I got here in time," he said.

Atkins gave a slow wink and a nod. "There should be enough for everyone."

When Hal had finished heaping his plate, Atkins set out the dishpan and served himself a plate of grub. By the time he sat down, Hal and Dane had exchanged what little information they had. Except for the clacking of spoons on metal plates, and the occasional stamp of a horse hoof, the camp was quiet.

Charley left first, announcing his intention to go relieve Diego. Dane sat on the ground a while longer, rolling a cigarette and then smoking it as Hal ate his dinner. Dane smoked the cigarette down to a snipe, then pinched it and tossed it into the coals. He got up, carried his plate and spoon to the dishpan, and turned his attention to the fire.

"I think the coffee should be ready," Atkins said. "If you want, you can take it off the fire and let it set for a minute or two."

Dane did as the cook suggested, then stood with his thumbs in his front pockets as he gazed out across the prairie.

When Atkins finished eating, he got up and put his plate and spoon in the dishpan. Lining up three cups, he poured them full of coffee. Dane took two cups, carried one to his brother, and sat down where he had been sitting earlier. Atkins carried his own cup to his former seat and joined the boys.

The three of them drank coffee for a couple of minutes without saying anything until Dane spoke. "The hell of it is, you know someone has been up to somethin', and there's no way to prove it." He looked at Atkins. "Someone's got a slick way of doin' things. Everywhere we go, there seems to be just a few less head of ours than there ought to be."

Atkins nodded. "Unless you can catch somebody red-handed, all you've got is a suspicion, even if it's a damn good one."

Hal spoke up. "It's hard not to think that we had a stool pigeon here. Not that any old fool couldn't run off a few head of cattle. But someone with a little inside knowledge could do a neater job of pickin' off just the right amount."

Atkins had a flickering image of an unshaven, walleyed puncher with whelks on his neck and a half-smile on his face, looking over the NB herd and keeping a running inventory on what was where.

Dane troughed a cigarette paper and shook tobacco into it, then pulled the drawstring with his teeth and slipped the cloth bag into his vest pocket. "Well, some sons of bitches think they're downright clever. But we'll catch 'em at it sooner or later, and they won't feel so smart then."

Hal twisted his mouth and nodded, as if he enjoyed the prospect of getting even. Atkins took note of the gesture. Hal, who was always so easygoing and willing to let Dane take the lead, seemed to be taking offense on his own behalf. As well he should, thought Atkins. The young man not only had a half-share in the ranch, but he also had an up-and-coming family to look out for.

As Dane finished rolling his cigarette and lit it, Hal brought out his clasp knife and took to cleaning his fingernails. The two brothers passed the next little while that way, sipping on coffee from time to time and making small talk about where they would ride that afternoon. After several minutes, Hal folded his knife with a click and put it away. Dane looked at his cigarette, stood up, and threw the stub into the fire pit. Hal got up also, and the two of them walked to their horses. With a quick "See you later," they rode off in the direction of the horse herd, where there would be fresh mounts for the afternoon ride.

A little while later, Diego came into camp long enough to eat his meal and gulp a cup of coffee. Then he got back on his horse and rode out in the direction he had come from.

Alone again in camp, Atkins built up the fire with some dry, twisted branches of sagebrush. He made a small, quiet fire with not much crackling or smoke and not much smell. In a few minutes he had a renewed bed of coals, where he set the dishpan, half full of water.

He looked at the sun, which had moved across the top of the sky. The warm part of the day would last a few hours more, he figured, and then things would cool down with the fading of daylight. As long as the temperature didn't drop to zero or lower, the longer nights made for good rest. In a couple of days he would be back in the comfort of the bunkhouse, with a sheet-iron stove and a woodpile to ward off the weather to come. He nodded his head to either side. Everything happened in its own good time.

Little bubbles began to form on the inside bottom of the dishpan as the first wisps of vapor rose from the surface of the water. Using two pieces of folded cloth for hot pads, Atkins lifted the pan off the coals and set it on the tailgate. He rolled up his sleeves, then enjoyed the warm comfort on his hands as he began to wash the dishes.

When he was finished cleaning all the eating utensils, he carried the pan to the edge of the campsite to pitch the water. Out of habit he scanned the surrounding country as he moved out of the immediate area of the wagon. Off to his left, to the southwest, an object appeared on the landscape. He stopped as the image registered in his mind. It was a lone antelope, about a hundred and fifty yards out. It stood in profile, with its head turned in the direction of the camp. A small set of horns curved up in silhouette, above the shadowed face. It was an antelope, sure enough; it looked like a nice young buck.

Atkins bent at the knees, lowering himself to a squat and setting the dishpan on the ground as he kept an eye on the antelope. It was a reflex he had, to make himself look smaller and like less of a threat to an animal that was in the category of camp meat. Turning, he moved in a crouch toward the wagon. Then, when his shape would be absorbed by the larger shape of the wagon, he went around to the off side. Looking up over the edge of the wagon bed, he saw that the antelope was standing in the same posture as before. That was good. An antelope was a curious animal and liked to stand and stare.

Atkins reached into the wagon and drew out his rifle from the scabbard. Crouching again, he moved to the tripod, about five yards to the left of the wagon. The antelope was still looking his way. As Atkins brought the rifle around, everything came together in a moment. He knelt with his right knee on the ground, his left foot on the rock he had placed at the edge of the fire pit, his left elbow on his left knee, his left hand and the forearm of the rifle on the peak of the warm tripod, and his right hand snugging the rifle butt into his shoulder. He levered a shell into the chamber and lined up the sights on the front quarter of the antelope.

There was an instant in time when a man knew things were right, as his own breathing and heartbeat, the steadiness of his grip, and the concentration of his mind came together with the poise of the animal. He knew exactly the moment, or second, when he should shoot. Without a flinch Atkins squeezed the trigger; the gun fired, and the recoil gave a tight, satisfactory sensation.

The antelope crumpled to its front knees and then fell over, its white underside flashing as its legs flailed and then settled.

Atkins rose from his crouch and, satisfied that he had made a good shot, took the rifle back to the wagon and slid it into the scabbard. Then he walked out onto the prairie to drag back his an-

imal. The antelope did not move. Its white abdomen made an easy mark to walk toward, and
its immobility gave Atkins the good feeling that
things had gone right. It had been a perfect moment in time, completed with a shot that hit
plumb center.

Approaching the animal, Atkins took note of
details that showed everything was in order. A
trickle of blood marked where the bullet had
gone in through the right shoulder. The animal
lay motionless, its short, yellowish teeth bared
and its dark eyes clouded. The dull black horns,
short and unimpressive, would offer a handhold.
Atkins glanced at the rest of the body, which
looked clean and healthy. Grabbing a horn in his
right hand, he started dragging the animal back
to camp.

Making a good shot had given him a lift of
energy, and he felt strength in his arms and legs
as he leaned forward and pulled the deadweight.
Twice he stopped to change hands, but he did
not feel the need to take a rest.

Back at camp, he skinned the lower hind legs
of the animal and then lifted the carcass to hang
it on the side of the wagon, spreading the legs
and lashing each hock to a wagon bow. When he
was finished with hoisting the animal, he stood
back and took a breather. An antelope was not
a big animal, but deadweight was cumbersome.
Stringing up the young buck had called for ex-

ertion, and it made Atkins feel strong. He recalled Tincher's slighting remark from a few months back, and he raised his eyebrows. If Tincher thought that anyone with gray in his hair was washed up, he had another think coming.

Atkins straightened out the body as it lay against the wagon. He would have liked to hang the animal so that it would clear the ground and swing free of the sideboards, but he would make do with what he had. Using the smaller of the two knives he had sharpened earlier, he went about skinning the animal. Slipping the blade under the hide and cutting from the inside out, to get less hair on the meat, he cut a line from the left shank down to the groin and back up the right shank. Then he trimmed the skin away from each of the legs, exposing the pink-orange flesh.

He skinned the animal all the way down around the body, then used the bigger knife to cut off the forelegs and head. Resuming with the smaller knife, he cut open the cavity and rolled out the intestines. After trimming out the colon and bladder, he slashed through the diaphragm, reached in with both hands to pull up on the heart and lungs, and soon had a hanging mass of offal. With a few more strokes of the knife, he separated the innards from the carcass.

He straightened his back and took a moment's rest. He had made smooth work of his task, and now the meat would cool as the warmth of the day faded. It made a great difference with antelope to skin the animal as soon as possible, to let it cool. The meat came out a lot less gamy that way.

After dragging the hide and guts a good ways off from camp, Atkins washed his hands in the dishpan, which still lay out of the way on the ground, and went back to the carcass. It was already cooler to the touch. He used his knife to scrape away a few white hairs from the inside of the hindquarters. A young buck like this should make good steaks, well worth the little bit of trouble it took to get the meat hanging. It was a clean piece of meat, with little bloodshot or mess. It made a neat package, just like the process itself, from the moment he lined up the shot until now, when he had the smooth carcass firm beneath his hand.

Looking at the sun, he decided it was time to get started on the evening meal. He put some of the nondescript firewood on the coals, then used his hat to wave air onto the embers and coax a flame into springing up. Once the fire caught hold, he went about cutting up another chunk of beef for supper.

As the afternoon began to fade, the fire took on a cheery aspect, burning down to a bed of glowing orange. Atkins hung a Dutch oven over the coals and got another mess of cut-up beef cooking. Then he mixed biscuit dough and took out the other Dutch oven. He greased it, set it on the coals for a few minutes, and then laid the little balls of biscuit dough in it. After setting the flanged lid in place and giving it a quarter-turn, he heaped a few coals on top.

He was setting the second batch of biscuits on the coals when Hal and Dane came riding in. Not long after that, Charley and Diego came in with the horse herd. No one said much about the antelope. Meat hanging in camp was common enough. As long as there was grub and it was prepared by someone else, most riders took what they got and didn't jaw much about it. Tincher had always been ready with a comment, but the Norden boys and the other hands didn't talk much about the food unless it was to pass a compliment.

After supper, while Charley and the brothers drank coffee and Diego tended to the horse herd, Atkins washed the dishes. After he pitched the dishwater, he built up the fire again, this time with cedar. He started with a handful of splinters, which gave off a cloud of gray smoke as the flames got started. Then he laid on larger pieces. Within a couple of minutes, the fire crackled and wisps of black smoke rose on the air. Atkins liked the musty, aromatic smell of cedar, which seemed cozier as the evening drew in.

The firelight flickered on the faces of the three young men—Dane with a brooding frown, Hal with a smile that told of faraway thoughts, and Charley with a relaxed expression. Atkins sat down by the fire also, and after yawning, he said, "Hal, do you know any good stories?"

Hal shrugged. "Not any I can think of right now. Not any good ones, anyway."

Dane nodded and threw a pinch of grass at the fire.

Atkins looked at Charley. "How about you?"

The young man tipped his head to one side and was silent for a moment. Then he said, "It takes me about half a day to remember one, and then nobody laughs."

Atkins looked back at the Norden boys and figured Charley knew plenty of stories but didn't think now was the time to tell one of them. "That's the way it is with me," Atkins said. As he hooked his arms around his knees, he remembered Tincher and the way he had of always trying to fill the silence. Atkins laughed to himself. Now that he thought of it, there wasn't really anything wrong with just sitting and looking at the fire.

Frost lay on the tarp when Atkins poked his nose out of his bedding. He hated to have to roll out in the cold morning and build up the fire, but it was his job to do it. As he lay there huddled, appreciating the last few minutes of warmth, he rehearsed the sequence of tasks he had to go through—expedite the fire, get the coffeepot go-ing, cook breakfast. He thought about the ante-lope hanging on the side of the wagon, and he imagined the cold night air had done a good job of chilling it.

Before long he had the fire going and flapjacks browning in the skillet. The sky began to pink in the east, and what had started as a cold, dark day gave way to warmth and daylight. As the men gathered around the fire, Atkins felt a tone of cheerfulness in the air. They had slept their last night out in the open for this season, and before the day was over they would be headed back to the ranch. The prospect of a comfortable bunk—or, in Hal's case, of charming company—no doubt picked up their spirits.

When the riders had set out on their separate ways, Atkins went about his chores of washing the dishes, stowing the bedrolls, and getting the wagon ready to move camp. He had just gotten the antelope wrapped in a piece of canvas when Diego brought the horses. In a matter of minutes they had the team hitched up and headed out across the prairie. Diego went back to the herd and brought it along behind as Atkins drove to the next campsite. He had chosen the spot be-cause he had used it a little while back, and he knew it would serve their needs.

He reached the new camp at midmorning, see-ing the fire pit still intact. A trickle of water ran in the creek, and he would be able to find firewood within a short walk. Diego took the wagon horses back into the herd and moved them all out to graze, leaving Atkins to set up his camp again. He didn't take long to lay things out, as he wanted to work on the antelope and get some of it ready for dinner.

Laying the carcass and the piece of canvas in the shade, he cut out the backstraps. The meat had firmed up nicely and was cold down to the bone. Might as well eat the best part first, he thought, while everyone was still around to enjoy it. After lifting out the choice cuts, which were about two feet long, all lean meat with no bone or fat, he cut them into steaks about three-quarters of an inch thick. Then he remembered to cut out the tenderloin, the small, tender strips that lay along the backbone, inside the ribs. When he had that task done, he looked at the sky; figuring he had another hour, he went about boning the front and hindquarters. What little meat was on the rib cage would go to the magpies and coyotes, he thought, so he carried the skeleton and leg bones out away from the campsite.

He preferred to cook antelope meat in an open skillet. He knew that this meat, being cooled right away and then separated from the bone, would be mild to the taste. When he held a cold steak up to his nose, it smelled as clean as deer meat. If it had any wild taste at all, cooking it in an open pan would make it milder.

When the sun was straight up, Atkins had both twelve-inch iron skillets on the coals, with the loin steaks sputtering in bacon grease. The day had warmed up but still had a little snap to it, so the smell of frying meat carried on the air. When Dane and Hal came riding in and tied their horses to the front of the wagon, they both showed interest in what was cooking.

The steaks were still raw-side-up, with the blood coming to the surface. Atkins used his long-handled, two-tined fork to turn the steaks and settle them in place. Finishing with that little task, he looked up to see Charley coming into camp on a trot. Ahead of the horse and rider came a yearling heifer, lanky with a set of horns almost a foot long on each side. Atkins knew Charley could rope, and rope well, so he imagined the puncher had hazed the heifer into camp because he wasn't sure if he should throw a rope on her.

"I can't see a brand," he said, "but I thought I'd check with you fellas."

Dane looked at Hal and nodded, and the two of them headed for their horses. In one smooth, continuous motion, each of them untied his horse, mounted up, turned out of camp, and untied his coiled rope.

"We'll get 'er," Dane said.

Charley nodded and stopped his horse.

Hal spurred his horse out first and put the heifer on a run. He swung his loop up and around and then snaked it out at the running animal.

Atkins could tell, by the way the horse turned and slowed, that Hal had caught the horns. As Hal took his dallies around the saddle horn, Dane came up on the other side of the heifer and threw his loop at her heels. His horse stopped short as Dane took his wraps, and the hind legs of the heifer stretched out behind her. In the same instant, Hal turned his own horse around, and the two brothers had the animal stretched out and holding still.

It was all done in a moment, smooth from beginning to end. In spite of a little dust rising, it was a clearly etched scene. Everything else in the world fell away and there was this, the Norden boys roping the head and heels as slick as any pair of cowboys on the range. Atkins knew that some of the good feeling was linked to a time when he would have been one of the two riders.

"Let's take a look at her, Charley." Dane's voice carried on the brisk air.

Charley rode forward and swung down, then walked toward the heifer with his reins in his right hand. With his left hand he rubbed against the nap of the hair on the animal's hip. "I don't see anything," he said.

Atkins imagined that if the heifer had no brand at all, Dane would slap the NB on her. It would be the only animal they branded on this outing, and not in strict accordance with the practices of organized roundups, where reps from other brands had the chance to look on. Still, if she didn't have a brand, Dane was likely to want to get something for all their efforts of the last few days. It was up to him.

Dane looked at the heifer as he spoke. "No tellin' where she come from."

"She was on her own," Charley said, running his hand up her side to the front quarter. He rubbed his hand back and forth on her shoulder. "Ah, here it is," he said. "Just a slash and a dot, it looks like. I don't remember seein' that one."

"Neither do I," said Dane. He looked at Hal, who moved his head in the negative. Dane urged his horse forward and shook some slack into his rope. "We'll let her go, then."

Hal moved his horse forward then, too, and Charley plucked the loop off the heifer's horns. She was free before she knew it.

"Let's run her on out of here a ways," said Dane, coiling up his rope.

Charley stepped back to his horse and swung aboard, and the three riders pushed the heifer out onto the range. After about fifty yards, Hal stopped and finished coiling his rope while the other two ran the heifer out another couple of

137

hundred yards. It had all been done in a matter of minutes, and if the animal carried someone else's brand, it was just as well that no one had a rope on it for very long.

By the time the three young men had their horses back in camp, the blood was barely coming up on the browned side of the meat. Atkins turned the steaks again, to let them cook another two or three minutes. The aroma of seared meat rose from the skillets, an encouraging smell that blended with the fragile, warm afternoon. Atkins was aware of a feeling that this was life on the range at its purest—good weather, a good camp, good horses, and cheerful young cowpunchers. It lifted a man's spirit and kept his heart young.

The mild weather ended not long after the crew made it back to the bunkhouse. Diego and Charley left for the winter, Laurel came back from town, and the ranch seemed to close in under the cold weather and biting wind. Atkins spent at least an hour of each day managing the woodpile, always trying to keep a day or two ahead of what he needed at the time. He didn't mind going out to chop wood or fetch back a few armloads, but he didn't mind the long hours in the bunkhouse, either. It was a time to relax, to let his thoughts stretch out. Dane spent some of his free hours at the little house, playing cards with Hal and Laurel. When he was at the bunkhouse, he didn't talk all that much. As the evenings wore on, Atkins remembered other times and other places when a cat or a dog had filled up the empty corners. The more he thought about it, the more he thought it would be nice to have a cat, for company if nothing else. It would add something to the feel of the place.

Atkins and Dane had been back in the bunkhouse for about a month when Hal came in one night just before bedtime and said he needed to take Laurel to town. He thought the baby was on the way. Dane jumped up and pulled his hat and coat off the wall. He was ready to go in an instant. Atkins asked what they thought he should do; after a short moment, Dane said he could stay and look after things. Atkins nodded, and the two boys went out into the night.

For a couple of days Atkins was on his own, with just the horses and the woodstove to keep him occupied. On the third night after the boys had left, Dane came back.

Atkins was standing at the kitchen stove, where he had a tea kettle boiling so he could steam and shape his hat brim. The smell of warm, damp felt hung in the air like the odor of a wet wool garment drying in front of a hot stove. Winter nights gave themselves to tasks such as shaping a hat or sewing a pocket onto a shirt, and with no sense of urgency, Atkins had gotten

139

the kettle going and had puttered with the hat brim.

Dane came to stand by the stove, where he took off his gloves and held his hands over the warm stovetop.

Atkins, with the hat in his hands, looked at Dane sideways. "I'd guess there was news."

Dane sniffed and held his head back, as if he was trying not to show any emotion. "There is. Laurel had a baby boy, and they called it Dane."

Chapter Eight

Atkins took the bridle from inside his coat, where he had stuffed it to keep the bit warm. Standing next to the stocky brown horse, he raised his right arm up and over the ears while with his left hand he guided the steel bit into the horse's mouth. He ran his thumb down the shank of the bit, the sidepiece that was shaped like a woman's leg, then straightened out the bridle, snugged the straps, and buckled the throat latch.

As he led the horse out into the cold, sunny morning, he hoped the good weather would hold. The air was still chilly at midmorning, but the sky was clear and the wind had not picked up. It looked like a good day to go to town, but he knew bad weather could roll in on any day.

Dane was waiting, already mounted on a large

141

sorrel horse. When Atkins swung into the saddle and gathered his reins, he looked at Dane, who nodded and turned to put his horse into motion. The two men rode out of the ranch yard, with the little house on their left. Atkins followed Dane's glance to the front door, then looked ahead again, feeling a twinge of guilt. Hal and Laurel shouldn't have to feel they were under anyone's eye.

Out on the trail, Dane was as taciturn as usual. It didn't seem to Atkins that Dane fell into somber moods; rather, he came out of them once in a while, not very fast and not for very long. It didn't bother Atkins. He had ridden and worked with all sorts of men, and he could take Dane's silence at least as well as he could tolerate the stream of stories and small talk he heard from others.

It had been a while since Atkins had gone to town or heard any real news from the outside world. Through the latter part of the summer and the early part of the fall, he had heard scraps of story about Cattle Kate. Back in July, a handful of cattlemen had hanged her and her companion, a fellow named Averill, over by Independence Rock on the Sweetwater. The cattlemen claimed that the two were rustlers, but common talk among the small-time operators and working men said that Kate, or Ella, did not have to go out and rustle calves. Many a happy cowboy brought her an animal and went away satisfied. Talk also had it that Averill had no cattle at all but knew a lot about land claims, and at least one of the cattlemen had laid an unjust claim to some prime meadowland. After two inquests and then a convening of the grand jury, with all witnesses having disappeared in the meanwhile, the case seemed to have been dropped. It looked as if money and power had won out, as if the cattlemen who were well connected did what they wanted and got away with it.

Atkins and Dane rode out north through the gap in the hills and onto the plains. The ride to town was a little longer this way, but Dane wanted to keep an eye out for NB cattle on this side of the hills. Before turning east, Atkins took a glance off to the west, where Silver Mountain rose dark above the plain. He wondered if Fey was staying for the winter.

Clouds of steam rose from the horses' nostrils. The animals moved at a good fast walk, giving an occasional snort or a shake of the head. Atkins looked at the landscape ahead of him, where the plains stretched away for miles. Old snow lay in a thin blanket everywhere, and despite the sun, Atkins knew he was in the middle of a cold expanse. It was good to have a sturdy, capable animal like a horse, which kept its head up and just walked on. A horse made a great ally against cold and distance.

It was nearly noon when the two riders came to the main street of Farris. Up ahead on the left, a figure sat on a bench in front of Chapman's store. From the hunched and bundled posture, Atkins figured it was Ev Mason, taking in what warmth he could get out of the winter sun.

"Did you want to stop at the mercantile, Dane?"

"Not right now. Maybe later."

Atkins glanced at the street ahead and then at Mason. "I think I'll swing over and say hello to Ev for a minute. Go on ahead if you want."

"I think I will. I'll be in the Elkhorn." Dane touched his spurs to his horse, and the big sorrel moved away in a trot.

Atkins turned in toward the hitching rail in front of Mason's bench. He gave a preliminary wave, and Mason, bundled in a gray overcoat and a fur cap, raised a gloved hand in return. Thinking it would be good manners to dismount rather than look down on the man, Atkins swung from the saddle into the street and then stepped up onto the sidewalk.

Mason lifted his head, showing his pale eyes and bitter smile. "Hello, Tom. Long time, no see."

"Hello, Ev. I thought I'd stop for a minute and hear a good word or two."

Mason had grown a scruffy beard, which moved as he turned his mouth downward in a scowl. "You won't get it from me." Then his face lifted back into a tight smile as he nodded backward and to the right, his drab brown hair folding against the collar of his coat. "There's always a good word of cheer inside, though." He drew his lips over his teeth, then said, "For a small price, of course."

Atkins laughed. "I suppose so." He glanced at Mason's crutches and then back at the man. "Any good news?"

Mason shook his head. "Only good news I've heard in the last month was the Nordens had a baby."

Atkins blinked at the choice of words. "I did hear about that," he said. "That's about it, then?"

Mason gave a couple of slow nods.

Atkins lifted his head a little. "I thought there might have been something else about those fellas that hung the woman over by Independence Rock."

Mason shook his head again. "No, I think that's all done with."

"No new scandals?"

The man on the bench patted his left leg, just above the knee, not far from where the leg ended. "I haven't started any, and I haven't heard of any."

"Maybe there aren't any."

Mason gave his bitter smile again. "None that anyone wants to tell me about."

"By golly, Ev, you make me feel guilty. I feel like I should go out and do something and then come back and tell you about it."

"Don't do it for me, Tom. Do it for someone who'll get some good out of it."

"Do you mean the thing itself, or the gossip?"

"Either one, Tom. Either one."

Atkins gave a light laugh, and after a few more words he said so long to Mason and walked his horse down the street. He found Dane standing by himself at the bar in the Elkhorn.

"What's new with your friend Mason?"

"Not much. Just his regular pint of bitters."

As Dane looked down at his whiskey glass, Atkins looked around the saloon. Half a dozen men stood along the bar, and that many more sat at a card table.

"Do you want a drink?"

Atkins wrinkled his nose. "No hurry." After a moment's hesitation he spoke again. "Did you have anything in mind for this afternoon?"

Dane shrugged. "Not much. I guess at some point in the afternoon we want to get fed, get wet, and get back home."

Atkins understood that getting wet meant more than just having a drink. "All of that sounds fine," he said.

"I'm not that hungry yet," Dane commented,

"but I'd just as soon not hang around in here."

Atkins had a passing thought, an image of rustling garments and light laughter. "Well," he said, "we could see about it."

As Dane tipped up his glass, Atkins looked around the saloon again. This time, now in clearer view at the end of the bar, he saw two men he recognized. The first flicker of recognition came from a dark, charcoal-colored hat with a broad brim and flat crown. Beneath the hat moved a pair of dark eyes with puffy lower eyelids. It was Fey, engaged in what looked like a cheerful conversation with another man—a man with a rough face and blurry eye, a man who showed a gap in his teeth when he laughed, as he now did.

It was all the perception of a few seconds, but it was a scene that held together and made sense as Atkins turned his back on the bar and walked away. Both Fey and Tincher were spending the winter in this country, probably in the same bunkhouse. What made as much sense as anything was the easy, familiar manner that hung in the air between the two men. It was not a surprise to see them together, and it was not much of a surprise that Dane didn't want to be in the same saloon with them. If there was anything odd at all, Atkins thought as he reviewed the scene, it was a note of cheerfulness in Fey. Maybe that was a good sign; maybe he didn't care if Dane was down the bar a ways.

Atkins and Dane had to wait a little while in the parlor until four girls came in. One was Dolly, whose blue eyes landed on Atkins right away. He nodded to her, and she came and sat by him on the divan, where he sat with his hat on his right knee. The other three girls did not get much of his attention, but he was pretty sure he did not see the dark-haired girl that Dane had paired up with the time before. All three were rather common-looking, full-figured but not shapely. Two of them left as a brown-haired girl sat down next to Dane on the other couch.

Dolly put her right hand on Atkins's left leg. He could tell things were going to be all right today.

"It's nice to see you again," she said.

"It's nice to be here."

"I thought you would have come back sooner."

"Oh, it was a busy season, and when we did get to town, we didn't stay long."

"That's too bad."

Atkins looked at her sparkling blue eyes and said, "It was, then."

She patted his leg. "That's right."

He could smell her perfume, could feel her vitality as she leaned toward him. "Uh-huh," he said. "Everything's fine today."

A voice rose up from the other couch. "Just don't call me Sugar Tit!"

"I didn't."

"You were about to. You called me Sugar."

"That's not the same."

"I could hear it coming. I know how you all talk. There's probably been three cowpunchers try to call me that in here."

"Well, I'm sorry."

Dolly reached around and put her hands on Atkins's ears, pressing her bosom against him as she did so. "Be careful," she said to the other two. "I don't want this boy to hear such vulgar talk."

Atkins smiled, appreciating the presence of a woman so close.

The other girl looked around. "He doesn't look like he just fell off the turnip wagon."

"That's just what you think," said Dolly, pressing his chin against her bosom. "He's my innocent little boy, and I have to take care of him."

"Well," said the other girl, turning back to Dane but speaking loudly enough for everybody's benefit, "just don't call me Sugar Tit. My name's Camille."

Dolly released her hold on Atkins but did not move very far back. "Such language. I need to get you away from it."

"I think it would be the best thing."

149

Once they were in the room and she had made her inspection, everything was as soft and gentle as before. It was as if no time had passed since the last time they were together beneath the wool blanket and cotton sheet. He remembered their conversation from before, and he thought again of how good it was to be able to do these things.

"I'm glad you look out for a boy like me."

She put her warm hand on his bare left leg. "I think a boy needs it, doesn't he?"

He rested his head against her breast. "I should say so."

On the ride back to the ranch, Dane didn't have much to say. He had come back out to the parlor after Atkins did, so he must have gotten his money's worth. Atkins did well enough at not speculating on the details, but he did wonder if Dane wished he had picked one of the other two girls instead. Camille. That was a name from the theater. He could imagine her growing up with the name Madge, in a godless household in St. Louis. Yes, that would be about right. That was where Tincher said he had some of his exploits.

Atkins brushed Camille and Tincher out of his thoughts and reflected again on the soft pleasures he had had with Dolly. It was too bad a sweet girl like her ended up in a life like that, but as long as men were willing to pay for such a thing—and they had been for centuries, as he heard it—there would be women to fall into it. Regardless of what being in that line of work meant in her life, which was a subject they wouldn't have gotten anywhere near, it was at least nice to meet a girl like her who had a good nature.

He had heard of men who had taken women out of those places and married them, but Atkins had never met a girl like that who held his interest. He still did not know, or had not decided in any definite way, whether he would ever get married. He thought he might, and at this late date he imagined it would not be with a young girl coming straight out of her parents' house. He had known a couple of girls like that, earlier, much earlier, but he was sure the time had passed for that possibility. If there should be a woman in his life, he imagined she would not be innocent, either—maybe not un-innocent in all the same ways, but she would have some chapters of her life already done.

Life at the ranch went on as it had, with the cold weather and short days of December. Hal and Dane rode out every day that the weather permitted, returning sometimes together and sometimes on their own. Hal often came to the bunkhouse after breakfast, when the day was just getting light. He and Dane would sit and drink coffee while Atkins cleaned up the dishes and the

151

kitchen. From their comments he gathered that they thought they might be able to catch somebody at something.

As part of his daily routine, after he had the kitchen in order, Atkins went across the yard to the woodpile. If he needed to cut or split more wood, he went into the toolshed for the ax and then warmed himself at midmorning with a bit of exercise. At about the same time, the Norden boys would go to the corral, catch their horses, and lead them into the stable. When they were saddled up, Dane would wait with the horses while Hal went into the little house for a minute. Sometimes Atkins saw Laurel standing at the open doorway and waving at the boys as they mounted up and rode away.

At other times, depending on how much work he had in the kitchen and how much wood he needed, he worked at the woodpile in the middle of the afternoon. He always had a sense of Laurel's presence, but as she had a little baby to take care of, it was rare that he would see her. Sometimes he heard the back door of the house open and close, but he did not often catch any movement at the front door. It was a peaceful coexistence, he thought. He did not trouble himself with wondering about what she might be doing, and he did not feel that she paid him very much attention, either. Still, it was reassuring to know there was another person nearby, and he imagined she felt the same at times.

The days wore on in this way until December 22, the day after the shortest day of the year. Atkins had fixed a beef stew and a plate of biscuits. Dane came in hungry just before sundown, so Atkins served the evening meal early. When it was done, he cleared the table and cleaned up the kitchen while Dane rolled and smoked a couple of cigarettes. The evening seemed to be settling into its routine when a knock sounded on the door. Atkins and Dane exchanged a glance. Hal didn't knock.

Atkins went to the door and opened it, and there stood Laurel, with a raw, worried look on her face.

"Come on in," he said, ushering her back into the eating area where it was light and warm. "What's the matter?"

Dane was up and out of his seat. "What is it? What's the matter?"

Laurel blinked her eyes and stood for a moment, as if she was getting used to the strange setting of a smoky bunkhouse. "Hal hasn't come back yet."

Dane's hand went up to his forehead. "Oh, my God. Are you sure?"

Laurel's eyes seemed to contract. "Of course I am. He always comes straight to the house."

"Oh, my God." Dane turned, looked at his

coat as if he thought of going out, and then
turned back to face Laurel. "I figured he'd come
in on his own, like he always does." He shook
his head. "It's been dark for over an hour."

Laurel nodded. "I know. I've been waiting for
him. I hoped I'd find him here, but I didn't really
think I would."

Dane looked back and forth between Laurel
and Atkins. After a deep breath he said, "I guess
I'd better go out and look for him. There's not
much of a moon, but at least I could try."

Laurel nodded.

Atkins could tell she was worried sick, and he
remembered the baby. "I suppose you need to
get back to your house," he said.

Dane took his hat and coat off their pegs and
turned back to Laurel. "Would you like it if Tom
went back and sat at your place, at least until I
got back?"

Laurel bit her lip and nodded. "That would be
all right."

"Do you mind, Tom?"

"Not at all." Atkins went for his own hat and
coat. In another moment he was out in the cold
night, walking Laurel back to her house while
Dane went to the stable.

Dane was gone almost four hours. He came
back in at about ten with nothing to report. The
men decided they would both sleep on the floor
in the little house. As he went to the bunkhouse

for the bedrolls, Atkins thought it would be better in the eyes of all concerned, including Hal if he should happen to come in during the night, if both he and Dane stayed over.

Daylight broke gray and cold, with still no sign of Hal. Atkins had slept very little, and he imagined the others had done the same—except for the baby. It was a quiet one, for as much as Atkins knew about babies. It had not cried the evening before, and except for a couple of brief squalls, it had not cried during the night.

At breakfast, Atkins agreed to stay with Laurel while Dane rode out again in search of his brother. It was a cheerless meal. Dane spoke matter-of-factly about the things that might have happened—getting thrown from the horse, having the horse go lame, trailing something too far and getting sidetracked, then having to spend the night out in an open camp. Even as Dane talked, Atkins knew they were all fearing the worst.

Dane came back at about noon, with a look on his face that prepared the others for the news. "I found Hal," he said. "It's not good. Laurel, I know this is hard, but I need Tom to go with me in the wagon. We'll be back before dark."

Atkins went outside and left the other two by themselves for a few minutes. Then Dane came out of the house, and the two of them went to the stable to hitch up the wagon. Hal's horse was standing inside. It was a little sorrel horse, one of half a dozen that Hal rode. Now it stood with an empty saddle, and Atkins felt a knot in his stomach.

"About five miles south of here," Dane said. "A little farther west than I thought he might have been."

"You don't think the horse threw him?"

"I don't think so. Not that one. And it hadn't gone far. It was just a couple of hundred yards away, grazing."

Atkins looked at Dane. "What do you think happened?"

Dane had a hard look on his face. "It looks as if he got hit on the back of the head."

As Atkins rode south in the wagon with Dane, he felt a numbness such as he had felt before, a strangeness that set in when the person who died was someone close. Even the familiar details of the world seemed disconnected. This was the NB wagon, half Dane's and half Hal's, and now Hal would never see it again. Nor would he see the prairie they rolled across—not now, in the cold of winter, and not in the warmth of summer when the NB cattle were fattening up. All of the things that Hal knew—his ranch, his horses, his friends, his brother, his wife and baby—would go on without him. Everyone had his own world, it seemed. Hal's was gone, and Atkins felt out of touch with his own.

* * *

Dane's guess turned out to be accurate. When they took the body to town, the sheriff and undertaker made the same assessment. A single blow to the back of the head had done it. The coroner thought a heavy object might have been used, but he could not rule out the possibility that Hal had fallen from his horse.

"That horse didn't buck," Dane insisted.

"Maybe not," said the coroner. "Maybe it never did, and maybe it did just once. I wasn't there."

"Neither was I," said Dane. "And the horse can't talk."

The sheriff came by the ranch the next morning, and Dane rode out south with him. They were back before noon. The sheriff declined dinner, saying he needed to get back to town, so Laurel, Dane, and Atkins sat down to another gloomy meal together. Dane gave a summary of the sheriff's investigation, which entailed riding out, riding a few circles around the scene, kneeling on the ground where the body was found, and making a few notations in a pocket notebook.

"So what does he think?" asked Laurel. Her face was drawn and pale, but she was finding something to hang on to.

Dane shrugged. "He thinks about the same as the coroner does. It could have been an accident, or it could have been something else."

Something else. Atkins poked at his potatoes. It was easy enough to imagine a two-man job, one holding a gun and the other aiming the blow. "Well, it was one way or the other," he said.

"Yes, it was," Dane said. "And I don't think it was an accident."

Chapter Nine

Atkins held the pitchfork in his right hand and felt with his left, trying to find the two nails on the wall. Dark was closing in at the end of the day, and the darkness was thicker inside the stable. He located the two nails, touching each with a gloved finger, and set the steel head of the pitchfork to rest upright in its place.

Walking back outside, he glanced at the little house that sat dark at the edge of the ranch yard. Dane and Laurel would be back in a few days, but even then, Atkins supposed, his hand would be welcome in some of the daily chores. As he walked to the bunkhouse, he appreciated the faint glow in the window. He had left a lantern lit in the eating area so he would not have to

grope in the dark when he finished taking care
of the horses.

As he went from the semidark room with the
cots to the low-lit mess room, he heard a meow.
Sam was standing up in front of the sheet-iron
stove, arching his striped yellow back and
stretching his tawny legs.

"Hey, Sam," he said out loud. "Did you miss
me?" Now that he was on his own in the bunkhouse, Atkins enjoyed the company of a cat. In
addition, it gave him the opportunity to hear his
own voice once in a while.

He went to the kitchen and built up the fire in
the cookstove, then fetched the lantern and
turned it up higher. He decided he would grind
coffee while he waited for the stove to heat up.
After filling the hopper with coffee beans, he put
his left palm on the mound of beans and began
cranking.

Sam sat in the doorway between the mess
room and the kitchen, with his tail curled around
his yellow haunches. He looked up at Atkins
grinding coffee. He had a habit of watching the
man at his tasks. If it entailed meat, fat, or grease,
Sam had his head raised and his body poised.
Otherwise, he took in the spectacle with casual
curiosity.

It would be this way for another three months,
Atkins thought. Now that Dane and Laurel were
married, the boss of the NB would stay in the

little house for good. That was to be expected. For the first two months after Hal's death, Dane had kept his bedroll in the little house. From time to time he made comments indicating that he was bunked in the other bedroom, and Atkins knew it was not his business to think about things beyond that. Now it didn't matter.

Atkins sensed that Dane felt some measure of guilt for moving into his brother's place in the house as well as in the family. Dane's voice carried a defensive tone whenever he mentioned Laurel or the baby, and even when he made small, factual statements such as "I'll be over at the house."

There was no way out of that, Atkins supposed. If Dane was going to move his bags into the house, one of the bags would have to have some guilt in it. The rest of it was all right. Regardless of the degree to which Dane had been attracted to Laurel before, he had a good motive in wanting to provide for her and the baby. Atkins thought he could see it in Laurel, too. She looked as if she felt protected. The past two months had taken some of the softness out of her. She looked stronger than she had when she and Hal were young newlyweds in love, but her face and gestures also hinted at deep fear. Atkins remembered the raw, wounded look she had borne when Hal was killed, and now it seemed as if the wound was closed over but not healed.

John D. Nesbitt

In the few times Atkins had gone to the little house to eat supper, he thought he saw the fear, and in the way her looks went to Dane, he thought he saw the comfort, the reliance on his protection.

Atkins put his hand over the cookstove. It was warming up pretty well. He looked at Sam and smiled. "Pretty soon. When I eat, you eat."

He put an iron skillet on top of the stove, spooned in a little bacon grease, and went to the closet where he kept the chunk of beef out of Sam's reach. He cut off about a pound of shoulder meat and cut it into smaller pieces, then put it sputtering in the pan. He looked at Sam and smiled as he pointed both ways with the fork. "You and me." Sam's head cocked about two degrees.

Atkins went to the shelf and took down a can of tomatoes. One thing about being a ranch cook was that a fellow didn't go hungry. For his own part, Atkins didn't care for a diet that was all grease and flour and spuds. Fresh meat and canned tomatoes were good for the health. They helped a fellow keep from catching colds and getting sores in the cold weather. Sam didn't care about tomatoes or biscuits or coffee. That was all right, too. A fellow knew how to look out for himself.

When the meal was ready, Atkins set the fried meat, the open can of tomatoes, and a plate of

162

cold biscuits on the table. Sam sat by the sheet-iron stove and watched him eat. The cat knew better than to crawl up on the table, and he knew, even deeper, not to get up on the cook-stove. Now he sat by the smaller stove and watched the man eat.

By the time Atkins finished his supper, the skillet was cool enough that he could scrape the grease and scraps into the cat's tin. Sam knew the skillet and the Dutch oven, and sometimes he stuck his head in the way and got a rap with the spoon, as he did now. He settled back and waited until his portion was served, and then he went at it. Atkins took the skillet back to the kitchen, where he washed it after the other dishes. When he went back to sit at the table, he missed Dane, sitting with his sleeves rolled up and a cigarette half-smoked. Atkins took a seat and looked around the room.

Sam was relaxed now, stretched out in front of the stove. Sometimes Atkins envied the cat and its ability to let everything go. With food in its belly and warmth at its back, it showed no awareness that those things had to be provided for or tended to. Nor did the cat show the slightest sense that a cold and hostile world waited outside. Yet the cat was no fool; it was always quick to spring into readiness, its muscles tense and its senses sharp. The cat's ability to release the tenseness and bring it back full at any

time impressed Atkins. Maybe it was because he
was a human, and maybe it was because he was
not young anymore, but he couldn't lie on his
back so vulnerable, as Sam was doing now, with
his legs sprawled out. Not in this life.

Dane and Laurel came back in the last week of
February. They had been gone two weeks, visit-
ing Laurel's sister Susie and her husband Ralph.
They had sold the barbershop in Farris and had
moved to Colorado Springs, where business was
supposed to be better. They couldn't get much
at all for the house, so they left it for Hal and
Laurel to use when they needed. Atkins imagined
that whatever deal they had would be renewed
with Dane. At any rate, Colorado Springs was
supposed to be a better place for business, and
it was farther south. When Dane and Laurel
came back, they said the weather had been
sunny. Laurel said Susie loved the baby, and
Dane nodded. They also said Ralph was working
in a good barbershop and would soon have one
of his own.

Atkins, with no one else to cook for until the
crew came back in May, was not expected to do
much more than keep the bunkhouse in order
and help with small jobs when asked. He did not
like sitting around, though, when he knew there
was work to be done, and even though Dane

wasn't much of a talker around his hired men, he seemed to appreciate the company.

Dane rode out almost every day, as before. To Atkins it seemed as if he was determined to catch someone at something or to find some evidence that would support his hunches. Atkins felt uneasy whenever Dane went out alone, and he kept an eye on the stable to see when the horse and rider came back.

One afternoon, close to dusk, when Atkins was across the yard fetching an armload of firewood, Dane came riding in. As he dismounted and led his horse into the stable, Atkins set down his firewood and went to the stable door.

"Hello, Dane," he said as he stepped inside.

"Evenin', Tom. What's in the wind?"

"Not much. Just thought I'd say hello."

"Uh-huh. That's good."

Atkins walked around the back of the horse to watch Dane, who had tied up the horse and unbuckled the rear cinch. "I had one thought."

Dane paused from pulling the front cinch loose. "Uh-huh. What's that?"

"Sometimes I don't talk to you for a whole day."

"Do you get lonely?" Dane smiled, as if it were a weak thing for a cowboy to admit.

Atkins laughed. "Not so much that. I ride out with you often enough, as far as that's concerned. It's not anything to do with cabin fever."

"Oh." Dane pulled the latigo loose and let the cinch swing down.

Atkins didn't feel as if he was getting much help. "I don't want to sound like your mother," he said, "but I think it would be a good idea if you checked in with me."

Dane had one hand at each end of the saddle, with his fingers hooking in to lift the pad and blankets with the saddle. He paused. "What do you mean?"

"Well, I mean, if you come in by yourself and you put your horse away, maybe you could just let me know. It would put my mind at ease."

Dane raised his eyebrows, looked sideways at Atkins, and then looked straight ahead at his saddle. "Seems like a bother."

"Maybe it is," Atkins said, and he could imagine why. Hal had never wasted any time getting back to see Laurel, and any man with a pretty wife could be forgiven for not wanting to stop and jaw with the bunkhouse cook. Beyond that, there was a matter of pride. A man like Dane would not want to admit he had an older man looking after him.

Dane pulled off the saddle, blanket, and pad, pausing long enough to flip the cinches up onto the top of the saddle. Then he carried the outfit to a wooden saddle rack, where he slipped the blanket and pad from underneath and set them, damp side up, on the saddle as he set it on the rack. He took a brush out of the tack box and walked back to the horse, glancing at Atkins without speaking.

"Maybe it is a bother," Atkins continued. "But like I said, it would put my mind at ease."

Dane was brushing at the damp saddle tracks on the back of the dark horse. Glancing at Atkins, he said, "Do you think I might not come back some time?"

"That's not exactly it. I just remember how hard it was on Laurel."

Dane stopped brushing for a moment and then went on. "If it's Laurel you're worried about, I suppose I should check in with her first, anyway."

Atkins felt himself getting impatient with Dane's stubbornness. "I don't know the best way to say it, Dane. But given what's happened, I don't like to have to sit around and wonder, and go out at night to count horses in the corral, and have Laurel be the one to have to come and knock on the door. Every time I don't know for sure that you came in, I have to think of those things."

Dane went around to the other side of the horse and started brushing from the neck back. "Then it's like I said. You think I might not come back some time."

Atkins shrugged. "Other things could happen. Even if your horse went lame, I would know to go out and look for you."

167

"Tom," said Dane with a steady look, "no sons of bitches are going to get me. For one thing, they don't have it in 'em. You saw how they were that day in town. They don't have the guts to face me, but they do to go after my little brother, because they knew he was weaker. And for another thing, it won't work with me. If I see one of those sons of bitches by himself, I can handle him, and if I see 'em both, they won't get a chance to get the drop on me."

That was as much as Atkins ever heard Dane say all at once. "So that's it, huh?"

"Uh-huh. That's it."

Atkins moistened his lips. "Well, you as much as admit there's cause for worry. You just don't want to do something that would show it."

Dane gave a short laugh and shook his head. "Look, Tom. I just don't see why I should have to check in with my aunt every time I put my horse away. I'm a grown man, and I've got someone else to check in with, anyway."

Atkins smiled. "All right, Dane. I think I understand. Let me try it this way. Blame it on me. Tell your wife that you have to keep your spinster aunt from worrying."

Dane shook his head. "It's still—"

"Look. You don't have to come by. I'll hang the triangle out here. I'm not using it now anyway. When you come in, just ring the bell. That way, Laurel will know you're here, and I'll know. Can you do that?"

Dane shrugged. "I guess so, but it still seems—"

"Tell her it's for your poor old aunt, Dane. She'll understand."

"Okay. You win, I guess."

Back in the bunkhouse, in the easy company of Sam the cat, Atkins stoked the fire in the cookstove. As he mixed up a batch of biscuit dough, the kitchen took on a warm, contented feeling. The smell of burning firewood contributed to the cheer, and before long it was blended with the savory smell of frying meat and then the powdery, airy aroma of hot biscuits.

As Atkins sat down to eat, he realized the talk with Dane had made him feel better. Admitting the danger was better than pretending it didn't exist. Atkins thought Dane might be a little too sure of himself, but it was hard to tell. Maybe he was trying to keep everyone else assured.

Whether he did or didn't have as much fear as he should, Dane was solid. He would stand up for himself and the others. Atkins had faith in that. He also thought, in less definable terms, that Dane would not let his brother's death go unquestioned. He believed Dane would not be satisfied with the routine investigation made by the law; he thought Dane would make someone accountable.

*   *   *

At the beginning of March, Dane and Laurel persuaded Atkins to take a little time off and go on a trip. He assured them he wasn't working too hard or suffering from cabin fever. To the contrary, he and Sam were taking it easy and getting along fine. Still, they said, he should get away for a little while and get everything off his mind. He was surprised to think he was that worried, and it made him wonder what signs he might have given. Then he realized that maybe Dane and Laurel just wanted the place to themselves for a little while. When he made a joking remark to that effect, they protested so much that he was sure he was right. So he packed his bag, rode a ranch horse into Wheatland, and took the train south. Diego had left an open invitation to come visit, and Atkins thought that would do as well as anything.

Diego's people lived in Pueblo, Colorado, south of Colorado Springs. It was plains country, not much different from the range up north, with mountains to the west and a broad, clear sky above. It was far enough south that the Mexicans weren't all shunted off into one corner of town. From the moment he stepped down from the train, Atkins saw dark-featured people at every turn and heard the soft, flowing syllables of Spanish.

Diego was happy to see him and proud twice

over—for having a guest to introduce to the family, and for having a family to receive the guest. The family house was an L-shaped affair, with various rooms showing signs of having been added on to the longer part as the family grew. Parallel to the long side of the house ran a row of sheds and chicken houses, with something of a courtyard in the middle. A fire was burning in one corner of the yard, up by the house, and perched above it, on a heavy grate, sat a sooty cauldron. A middle-aged woman was poking at the contents with a stick, and as Atkins and Diego waved, she lifted out a dripping mass of pale red fabric. It looked like long underwear.

At Diego's invitation, Atkins set his bag next to the house and took a chair in the yard, near enough to benefit from the warmth of the fire. The woman nodded and went about her work. After a few minutes, Diego came out with two cups of coffee. He pulled up a chair next to Atkins and sat down.

"Well," he said, "how's everything at the ranch? How are the boys?"

Atkins got through the hard part. He felt like the wise uncle, the one who was supposed to be strong and show understanding while the young man's eyes filled with tears.

The older woman asked Diego a question in Spanish, and he gave her a pained answer.

"O-o," she said. Then she looked at Atkins and said, "I am very sorry."

When the sad part had been gotten through, the visit began to take better shape. Diego said he was going to take the coffee cups to the kitchen and it would be a good time for Atkins to set his valise inside the house. As he did so, he met Diego's mother, who was peeling onions in the kitchen. He also met half a dozen kids—a mixture of brothers, sisters, and cousins. Two of the girls were sweeping the house, so Atkins followed Diego back outside. There he was introduced to Diego's aunt, the woman who tended to the laundry. She was a widow, Diego explained, and the two cousins inside were her son and daughter. As evening began to fall, an older man in work clothes and a winter cap came to the fire. Diego stood up and introduced him as his father. Atkins also rose for the introduction.

As they shook hands, the older man took his measure of Atkins and said, "My son, very good cowboy?"

Atkins smiled. "Yes, sir. He's a good cowboy."

The old man turned to his son and said something that had an authoritative tone to it. Atkins caught the word *cerveza,* and he knew things were getting better.

"You can go inside with my father," said Diego. "I need to go run an errand, and then I'll be back."

Atkins followed the father back into the house, which was clean and in order. Atkins gave a little effort to trying to keep the people straight. During the introduction, the father had given his name. Atkins thought the first name was Felipe, but he wasn't sure. His last name, like Diego's, was Hernández. Atkins got it put together, repeated it silently to himself, and thought it was right.

Atkins was left to sit by himself in a wooden armchair in the sitting room. He could hear promising sounds from the kitchen, and the smell of fried corn tortillas hung on the air. After about ten minutes, Diego came out of the kitchen with two tall glasses of beer. Then the father came in from the other side of the house, his face gleaming and his hair slicked back. He took a seat in a padded armchair, made a comment to Diego in Spanish, and called out to the kitchen. A minute later, Diego's mother brought the father a glass of beer.

"Pretty cold over there in Wyoming?" he asked.

"I'd say so. We've had cold weather this winter."

The older man smiled, showing a row of good teeth beneath his mustache. "Lotta cows, huh?"

Atkins nodded. "That's mostly it, where I live."

"Yeah. They got a lotta sheep there, too, don't they?"

"In other parts, they do."

"Yeah, that's what I thought. My brother's son, he works over there on a sheep ranch."

"Oh, really? In what part?"

"I don't know. It's over there in Wyoming."

"Oh. Uh-huh. And yourself? What do you work at?"

"I work for the railroad. Two of my boys do. But this one, he wants to be a cowboy. I tell him, 'Go be a cowboy, and when you get tired of that, come back here and get a good job on the railroad.' He knows it."

Atkins looked at Diego, who smiled.

"My father tells me I have to get it out of my blood."

"Do you think you can?"

Diego gave a sheepish smile. "Oh, probably. All my family is here. You know, you want to stay where your family is."

Atkins nodded and took a sip of his beer. The conversation had come to a lull, so he said, "Well, I got a cat since you left. I ended up on my own in the bunkhouse, so I got a cat. Cost me ten dollars, but he's a good one."

Diego smiled. "A cat, huh?"

"Yeah. A yellow one. His name is Sam."

Diego shook his head. "You watch out. Charley's gonna make a song about him."

They talked on for a while longer. Diego asked about Dane and Laurel and the baby, about the horses and the cattle. He asked about other people he knew from that country, but he never mentioned Fey or Tincher. All this time, the father sat in his chair and sipped on his beer.

Voices came from the kitchen, and the older man rose from his chair. *"Vamos,"* he said.

"Time for chuck," Diego said, smiling at Atkins.

The women served pork in a red chile sauce, with mashed beans and boiled rice on the side. Diego told him to dig in, so Atkins did. He helped himself to the flour tortillas that sat in a stack wrapped with a towel. When he had a good start on the meal, he realized that only the three men were eating. He asked Diego about it, and Diego said the others would eat afterward.

When the men were through eating, they went back to their chairs in the living room. The elder Hernández rolled a cigarette and smoked it, and Atkins enjoyed the tranquillity.

He spent three days with Diego and the family. On the second day they had a barbecue. Atkins watched as Diego greased the grill with lamb fat and then laid out the chops and ribs. The smoke and the sizzling fat and the cool taste of beer blended together to give Atkins a sense of contentment. The background conversation, in Spanish, made a soft melody. No one seemed worried. No one was on edge. They had a guest, and they wanted him to eat well, drink well, and sleep well. It was a good plan.

During the day, while Atkins and Diego sat around the house drinking coffee and not doing much of anything, even talking, various people came into the dining room to say hello. Among them were two young women in their early twenties who caught Atkins's attention. Diego introduced them as his cousins. They did not come together, and they looked a little bit alike, so Atkins wasn't sure how many times he had seen each of them. He thought they had both stopped in once each day. Atkins was embarrassed that he wasn't more attentive, but he had met so many people who came and went, and so much of the talk was in Spanish when people dropped in, that he couldn't keep everyone straight. He liked the two young women. They were pretty and polite and a little shy, staying only long enough to say hello.

After three days of sitting around feeling full as a pup, Atkins decided he had rested well enough. He thanked Diego and his mother, wished he had gotten to see the two young women one more time, and got ready to go.

Diego offered to go to the station with him. "Do you want to ride? We can send for a hack."

"Actually, I would just as soon walk, if you don't mind it."

And so they walked across town, about two miles, to get to the station. Atkins found himself in the midst of other pale-faced people now, and he felt the old world coming back.

"Well, thanks again, Diego. It was a good visit. I hope to see you in the spring."

"I hope so, too. And like my mother said, this is always your house here, so come anytime."

"Thank you. And give my thanks to your father as well. Oh, and also, say hello to your cousins."

Diego nodded. "Sure."

Afterward, when Atkins was seated in the passenger car and thought back on it, he realized Diego might have thought he meant the two little cousins, the children of the widowed aunt. He laughed to himself. Those young women were pretty, but there was no point in fooling himself. They were young and innocent; they had family and church and a full life right there. He was just an older man to them, someone not as old as their fathers but deserving respect. He imagined they all saw him as a nice *señor*. That was how he felt as the train pulled out of Pueblo—a nice man who used to be a cowboy and was going back to live with his cat.

It reminded him of something Diego had said. A fellow liked to be where his family was.

Chapter Ten

Atkins handed the hot iron to Dane. With his left foot planted on the calf's hip and a steady hold on the iron, Dane pressed the searing NB brand into the calf's flank. The smell of burning hair rose in the dusty air of the corral as the calf let out a bawl.

"That's one," said Dane. "Let 'er up."

Diego stood up and backed away from the front end of the calf, and Charley Porter moved in a crouch to let the hind end go free.

It was the first calf of the season to be branded. Dane had decided to run in a few head that were close to the ranch, about a dozen cows he had kept an eye on since calving. He said to hell with anyone else, he was going to brand these few that were beyond dispute. He was going to do it before anyone else could, and before the organized roundup began. Atkins imagined he had stewed on it all winter and had his mind made up. No one asked any questions when he told the boys what they were going to do. Because they were still at the ranch and Atkins didn't have a wagon to tend to, he had a few hours to spare. He rode out for the gather and now lent a hand for the branding.

Diego and Charley had both been back for a few days. Diego showed up first, looking about the same as he had when Atkins had seen him a couple of months earlier. Maybe there was a little less innocence than the year before—a little more seriousness in the brown eyes, a little more firmness in the smooth, youthful face with its clear tan complexion. At any rate, he was a year older, with a season's experience at horse wrangling plus a bit of cowpunching.

He made it known to Atkins that he wanted to learn how to rope and be a regular hand. Atkins, knowing that Dane would just as soon hire someone who already knew, decided he would help the young man if he could. When the first day's work was over and Dane had gone into the little house, Atkins took a rope from the wall. When he had the rope in his hands, he felt the old, familiar feeling. The hands worked almost by themselves, fingering the coils and shaking out a loop. He showed Diego how to swing a loop, rolling the wrist and then making the toss. Then he pulled a stump out of the woodpile and set it up by itself. It fell over each time Diego slapped the rope at it, and after a few tries, Diego asked about practicing on a corral post. Atkins explained that a fellow did most of his roping on horseback, except when he was roping out a horse to ride, and so most of the time he was throwing the rope down and not up. Diego gave a couple of brisk nods and went back to trying what Atkins had set up for him. By the end of the evening, he could rope the stump about once out of every eight or ten tries.

Charley Porter showed up the next day, riding the same dappled gray horse and wearing the same short-brimmed hat. The bandanna hatband was gone, but it was the same old Charley, all smiles and good nature. Some of the humor went out of him when he heard the news about Hal, but before long he was cheered up again, singing "Birdie in the Cage" to Sam as he scratched the cat's head.

Charley also had a guitar this time, a well-traveled instrument that he took out of a worn leather case. Diego asked him how long he had had it, and he said quite a while. Atkins wondered if it had spent a few months in a pawnshop in Cheyenne the season before, but then he wondered why he bothered to think about things like that. It didn't matter any more than the hatband did. It was good to have Charley back.

Neither of the hired hands made much mention of Hal, and the subject of his death did not come up. Atkins also noticed that in the frequent references to one thing or another that had gone on the year before, Tincher's name came up hardly at all. Atkins heard no mention of Fey, except on one occasion after supper the first evening, and even then the reference was indirect. Atkins was washing dishes in the kitchen while the boys sat around the table talking. Diego had just said something he didn't catch, and then Charley's voice came out clear.

"Fey-o. I know what that means. Ugly."

Both of them laughed, so Atkins supposed they were talking about horses or women.

Also on Charley's first evening back, he learned that Diego wanted to practice roping. He said he would be glad to show him anything he might know, and before long the two of them had ropes and were sitting side by side on the edges of their chairs, with their elbows on their knees and their forearms straight out, the coils in one hand and the loop in the other.

They started the branding the next day, and it went well enough. With each animal they branded, the men followed the same pattern. Diego and Charley on horseback cut out the calf from the holding pen and pushed it into the corral. Atkins worked the gate. With a little help

from the other two at hazing, Dane roped the calf.
The horse held the rope tight until Diego and
Charley had the calf on the ground. Atkins went
for the iron, and Dane put his brand on the calf.

They branded all the calves in one morning
and had them turned out with their mothers by
noon. Dane and Diego had already brought in
the horse herd, so the boys spent the rest of the
day brushing and combing the horses. For the
next two days they would be saddling them and
bucking out the ones that needed it. Charley was
the best at topping broncs, but he said he wasn't
going to do it all by himself. He said this at supper, when Dane was at his own house. He said
that in most outfits, each rider bucked out his
own string and that was it, but Dane hadn't
picked out which horses went with which man's
string. He said he didn't think Dane had decided
whether he should break up his brother's string
or turn it all over to one man.

"I think he should break 'em up and give a
couple of gentle horses to each of us, and spread
the others around, too. But it's his business. In
the meanwhile, though, we've got one big bunch
of horses that need to be saddled and rode. That
means you're gonna have to get on some of 'em,
Diego."

"How about Tom?" Diego's eyes flashed as he
smiled.

Atkins put up his hands. "I fill in. You need

another hand to ride out here and there, and I can do it. But my bronc-bustin' days are long over."

The two young men laughed.

In the course of his own daily work, Atkins went out to the corral from time to time. Most of the horses did not give much trouble, and Charley worked with the worst ones. Still, Diego got a few wild rides, lost his hat a few times, and got piled in the dirt at least twice.

Now that the weather was warming up, Laurel came out of the house for a little while each afternoon. Part of her purpose, Atkins supposed, was to give the baby a little fresh air and sunshine. She also seemed to take an interest in the work. Atkins imagined she had to be thinking of Hal, at least at times, as she watched the men go about the work that had been so much a part of his life.

After two and a half days with the horses, Diego and Charley went to work at getting the wagon ready. Atkins had them sweep out all the winter debris, knock the mud off the underside, and grease the axles. With Atkins's help they lifted up the chuck box, with the NB branded on its sides, and got it bolted into place on the tail end. They put the hoops into place and tied a long pole to each side. Still with Atkins's help they brought down the canvas sheets, one large one and two smaller ones, that had been rolled up and hanging from the rafters in the stable.

Next came the detailed work of loading the chuck box with all the items and accessories they would need for an extended outing. Getting everything that was necessary but keeping it to a minimum was always the trick. Everything had its place, and every little place was taken up.

Then came the grub. Atkins preferred to grind all the coffee ahead of time and double-bag it, so that no holes would wear through with the constant jostling of the wagon. He also double-bagged the flour, sugar, rice, beans, and dried apples, making sure it all got sacked and tied snug. When the boys tied the canvas down over the bows, Atkins looked inside. There would be barely enough room for four bedrolls. When they threw in with the other outfits, one of them would provide a bed wagon, but starting out, the NB wagon would be stuffed to the gills.

That evening, when all the work was done and the men lay relaxing on their bunks, Charley took his guitar out of its case. After some preliminary strumming and tuning up, he played a few songs that Atkins recognized from the year before. They were the same songs, but fuller now with the sounds from the guitar.

When there came a pause, Diego spoke from his cot, where he lay leaning on one elbow. "I told Tom you were probably gonna make up a new song."

Charley smiled. "You never know. Maybe I did."

"Already?" Diego's eyes widened.

"No, not since I got here. But maybe I did one or two over the winter, and maybe even one on my way here."

Atkins, with his hands joined behind his head, looked over to his left and said, "Why don't you try out one of 'em, then?"

Charley shrugged. "I guess I could. I haven't sung this one in front of anyone else before, but I could give it a try." Sitting up straight again on the edge of his bunk, he strummed his way into the melody. "I call this one 'Nebraska Girl,' " he said, and began singing:

"I've got a girl back in Nebraska
    With sparkling eyes and long, dark hair—
A voice that rings with golden laughter,
    And lips that brush away all care.

"When last I saw her in Nebraska,
    Beneath the springtime moon so bright,
She whispered words demure and tender,
    And held me in her arms so tight.

"The golden moon above Nebraska
    Lit up the prairie with its glow—
And showed to me a scene of wonder,
    A dark-haired goddess here below.

"I had to leave her in Nebraska—
  But I'll go back when roundup's done,
And meet her on the golden prairie
  Beneath the smiling autumn sun.

"And when the winter in Nebraska
  Gives way to prairie flowers in bloom,
We'll walk together, slow at sunset,
  And watch the rising of the moon.

"And when the moon above Nebraska
  Lights up the evening warm and free,
We'll pledge our love in moonlit whispers,
  My sweet Nebraska girl and me."

"That's a nice song," said Diego. "Is it true?"

"I guess it's as true as any song I sing," Charley answered. "But I wish it was all the way true, all the time."

"You mean you know a girl like that, but she doesn't care about you?"

"Oh, I think she does. Just not enough to make up her mind and get rid of a couple of other fellas that keep pesterin' her."

Atkins took the liberty of making a comment. "Well, I'm not an expert at these things, Charley, but maybe if you're gone she'll see how much she misses, and that'll be the end of your cow-punchin' days."

Charley twisted his mouth. "I don't even know about that. There's plenty of cows where she comes from, and I haven't been in many places where there wasn't."

The NB wagon rolled out early, just behind the horse herd, and made it to the first camp before noon. None of the other outfits had arrived yet. Atkins unhitched the horses, dropped the tailgate, and went about setting camp. Dane rode in on his own, leaving Charley and Diego to ride around the horse herd.

"I guess I'll just fix grub for the four of us, and then rustle up some more for the others if they haven't eaten when they get here."

Dane looked around from tying his horse to the front wheel. "I guess so," he said with a frown.

Atkins built up a fire and began slicing bacon. They would kill a beef when all the outfits were together, each one taking its turn at supplying an animal from its own stock. For the moment, he thought, it would be sure enough that as soon as he put on grub for four men, another outfit would roll in. When he finished slicing the bacon and laid it in the skillet, he went around to the front of the wagon and rooted behind the seat. He had one sack of spuds, and he might as well use them while they were good. He dug out four good-sized ones and was on his way back to the tailgate when he saw two riders coming from the west. Diego and Charley were east of the wagon with the horses, so these two riders, whoever they were, would come to the wagon first.

Atkins set down the four potatoes and brushed his hands on his apron. He didn't like the looks of the two riders, not even at a distance. From their outlines he was pretty sure they were Fey and Tincher. Dane had already seen them and was standing ready, facing them with his back to the wagon and his right hand hanging loose near his six-gun. He had rolled a cigarette a few minutes earlier, and he held it in his left hand. Atkins thought about his rifle, tucked down in the wagon beside the beans and rice, under a heap of canvas and bedrolls.

"You know who that looks like," Dane said.

"Uh-huh."

As the riders came in closer, there was no doubt. It was Fey on the left and Tincher on the right. Both of them rode dark horses, which made Atkins wonder if they had black slickers as well, for night work. He had a feeling of contempt for both of the men, but he knew his opinion didn't matter much. He would have to keep his mouth shut and let Dane do the talking. The good part was that he knew Dane despised the two at least as much as he did.

Fey and Tincher rode up to within twenty yards of the camp, well within the bounds of what was commonly understood to be the domain of whoever had the camp. Neither of the

men dismounted, which was a discourtesy in itself.

Atkins could see Fey well enough—the
charcoal-colored hat with the flat crown and
broad brim, the brown eyes with puffy lower eyelids, the straight hair sticking over his ears. He
wore a gray wool coat, probably the same one he
had worn on earlier occasions, with a holster
poking out below it on the right. The man had
his trousers tucked into his boots, and his silver
spurs caught the midday sun.

"Afternoon," said Fey, showing his teeth.

"Afternoon," Dane answered. "Did you drop
by to eat?"

Atkins hoped not, but it was the code of cow
country that anyone who rode up to the wagon
deserved an invitation. And the smell of frying
bacon was on the air.

"Not really. Mike here can smell grub a mile
away, so he'd probably like to take you up on it.
But we can't stay that long."

Atkins looked at Tincher, who hadn't changed
much. He wore the same dark hat with the band
of silver conchos around the crown. As always,
his face was ruddy and rough, and he looked as
if he hadn't shaved in a week. A dirty neckerchief
hung at his throat, and a smirk played on his face.
Tincher was wearing a brown sack coat that
came nearly to his knees and bulged where his
six-gun would be. Atkins wished he would open

189

his mouth and show the gap between his teeth, so Atkins could see everything he loathed about the man. But for once Tincher didn't speak.

Dane lifted the cigarette to his mouth, raising his left hand but not moving his right. As he blew away the smoke, he said, "Just bein' sociable again?"

Fey showed his teeth. "You could call it that."

"Uh-huh."

"You could call it a friendly visit, just to let you know that some of the others know—" Fey paused in his singsong.

"Know what?"

"That you got in a little branding ahead of time."

Dane took another drag on his cigarette. "Fey, I'll tell you this once, straight out, in front of your pal Tincher. I branded those calves myself, on my own land, in my own corral. Every damn one of 'em was with a mother that carried my brand. Now, unless someone has run off the mothers or done somethin' to them, there's nothing to dispute. So don't try to start something, even if you've got a smart one to back you up."

Atkins glanced at Tincher, who was still smirking but not looking very flattered.

"I'm not startin' anythin'," said Fey. "And as for doin' everythin' on the square, I'm sure you've got plenty of witnesses. Your funny uncle and the others."

"You know a lot, don't you? About my family." Dane tossed his cigarette into the campfire, and his left hand went down to his side in balance with the right.

"Not so much," said Fey. "I'm sure there's things I don't know."

Atkins had the feeling that Dane was digging while Fey was throwing dirt back into the hole.

"Yeah, and I'd bet there are things you do."

Fey showed his teeth and shook his head. "I don't even know half of what I seen. But I know there's a bunch of new calves runnin' around with your brand on 'em."

"I already told you once. There's nothin' to dispute on that."

"Sure, sure," said Fey. "You never done anythin' wrong in your life. Everyone knows it."

"Knows what?"

Fey smiled, this time keeping his mouth closed and spreading out his bristly mustache. "How clean you are." He put both hands on the saddle horn. "Why, anyone in town right now could tell you that."

Atkins thought for a moment about Laurel. Just the day before, while he and the boys were stocking the wagon, Dane had gone to town, rented a buggy, and moved Laurel and the baby into Ralph and Susie's vacant house. Atkins was sure that Dane's thoughts had flickered to the same place. Fey knew how to hit a nerve.

Dane's voice came out steady. "Fey, if you've got something to say about me, you ought to try saying it to my face."

"What is there to say?" Now he showed his teeth. "Like my pappy always said, if you can't say somethin' nice about someone, don't say anythin'." He raised his right hand and gave half a wave. "With me, nothin' but the best. I said you're clean, and everyone knows it."

Atkins moved to the fire to turn the bacon, and for a second everyone was silent. Then he heard Dane's voice.

"Everyone knows everything, don't they?"

Atkins glanced at Tincher, whose one good eye seemed to be gazing absently at Atkins's movements with the bacon and whose dull eye gave the impression that he wasn't thinking for the moment.

"Oh, I don't know," Fey answered. "There's probably not many secrets in this country. A man farts, and his neighbors talk about it."

"Uh-huh. But I'd bet there's some things that not everyone knows."

"Is that right?"

Atkins glanced again at Tincher, who hadn't said a word so far. His face was relaxed now, and he seemed to be studying the conversation.

Dane's voice came back. "That's right. There's things I don't know."

"Uh-huh. Like what?"

"Like where some of my steers went last fall. We seemed to come up awful short when it came to shippin'."

"Listen to you cry," said Fey. "Your herds grow faster than anyone's, and you say the country's full of rustlers."

Dane made a dry spit off to his right. "I said I came up short, and I know what I'm talkin' about."

"Yeah, yeah. Like you're the only one that ever lost a head of beef." Fey was making short, wavy motions with his right hand.

"And that's not all."

Fey's hands went together on his saddle horn as his face hardened around his broad hook nose. "Well, tell us the rest."

"There's another thing I don't know, and that's what happened to my brother."

Fey shook his head. "I was sorry to hear about that. Mike said he was the nicest sort of fella."

Atkins looked at Tincher and despised him for the look of pious innocence he had put on.

"I bet he did," said Dane. "Anyone should. But I'm not satisfied that I know what happened to Hal."

"Of course not. You're—"

"Don't give me your two-bit sympathy, Fey. I want you to know right now, in front of these others, that I don't think my brother's death was an accident."

Fey arched his eyebrows. "Well, if you think I know anything about it, you've got a long way to go."

Dane said nothing. He just looked at Fey and then at Tincher.

Finally Tincher spoke. "Dane, we had nothing against your brother. Everyone liked Hal."

Dane's eyes narrowed. "I didn't even know you were workin' for 'em then."

Tincher's face went blank and then he brushed his nose. "I didn't say I was. But I was eatin' their grub when I heard about it."

"That's the one part I believe," Dane said. "That you were eatin' their grub."

"Dane, if you think I had anything to do with—"

"Go to hell, Mike. I think you've got a pretty good idea of what I think." Dane turned to look at Fey. "Both of you. And if you think you can come into my camp and push me around about brandin' my own stock, you can go to hell a second time."

Fey and Tincher looked at each other, and then Fey looked back at Dane. "Well, I guess we said all we had to say. A little friendly observation was all. You know, all in a day's work."

The two men turned their horses and left the camp at a fast walk.

Dane took out his tobacco and papers and began to roll a cigarette. Atkins noticed a little quiver in his hands, but not much. Dane stuck the cigarette in his mouth, used the shovel to lift a coal from the fire, and lit his cigarette.

"Two-bit sons of bitches," he said.

"That doesn't mean they couldn't do something like that again, though."

"They'd need more nerve, Tom."

Atkins didn't say any more. He thought Dane could benefit from having a little more caution. Maybe in the public eye there wasn't much to fear about Fey and Tincher, but they might not always do their work when someone was watching.

After dinner, the other outfits still hadn't shown up. Diego and Charley stayed with the horses, and Dane said he was going to go out for a ride on his own.

Because just the two of them were at the camp, Atkins hazarded a comment. "Do you think that would be a good idea?"

"My God, Tom. Am I supposed to be too scared to go out on my horse? Especially at this time of the year, when the range is crawlin' with roundup crews?"

Atkins shrugged. "I guess not."

Dane untied his horse, tightened the cinch, and swung aboard. "See you at supper," he said, touching his spurs to the horse.

As Atkins watched him ride away, he let out a long breath. Dane wasn't all wrong, he thought. He could just use a little more fear.

Chapter Eleven

Atkins used the flat nose of the hatchet head to drive in the tent stakes. The thud of the steel head on the wooden stake end was the only sound for a couple of minutes until Dane spoke.

"This ridgepole fits together in three pieces, and it's notched on each end for the uprights."

Atkins rested the hatchet by his knee as he looked up. Dane had the ridgepole assembled with the hingelike brackets pinned together. It looked like good hardwood, the stuff of ax handles and wagon beams. Dane, who had just come back from Cheyenne with Laurel and the baby, had bought the tent, used, and wanted to take a look at it before he put it away for the winter.

"This is handy," he said. "If you camp in the mountains, you can always cut poles. But down here, you pretty much have to carry your own with you."

"Yeah, it's all right, as long as you have a wagon to carry it in." Atkins had seen all sorts of tents and shelters. This one was sturdy enough, but it was bulkier and took more time to set up than the little pyramid tents did, with their single upright pole.

"Oh, it's fine," Dane said. "And it was a good time to buy one, at the end of the season. And it's already got all the guy ropes for pulling out the sides by the eaves."

Atkins nodded and went back to pounding stakes. That was the way Dane was. If he decided how to do something, even if it was the hard way, he stuck with it and justified it. And it was not a bad tent. It was just that Atkins knew who was going to get the job of setting it up every time.

Overall, Dane seemed pleased with the trip to Cheyenne. He had brought back a good load of food supplies, clothing, kerosene, and odds and ends of small hardware. In addition, Atkins gathered, the visit had gone well with the doctor. Laurel hadn't started to show before roundup started—or at least Atkins hadn't paid enough attention to notice—but when the season was over, there was no doubt that she was in the family way again.

If Dane seemed satisfied, it was not with everything. Out on the range, Atkins had noticed a constant restlessness, the blue eyes always searching, it seemed, for telltale signs of missing steers and changed brands. Atkins also supposed he was always on the lookout for any details that would add to his understanding of how his brother died, but if any such details revealed themselves, Atkins was not aware of them.

When the two men had the tent set up and the sides stretched out, Dane went to get Laurel so she could see it. She would not have to walk far, as they had pitched the tent between the stable and the house. Laurel came outside, taking measured steps and squinting in the low sun of afternoon.

She said hello to Atkins as he stepped aside and held open the tent flap. She peered in, then stepped back and nodded.

"We could put a canvas floor in it," Dane said.

Laurel nodded again. Atkins tried to read the expression on her face, but he couldn't be sure. Her face seemed at once both soft and hard—soft with the extra flesh that a woman put on at times like this, and hard with a resistance to pain from the outside. It looked like a hardness that was there to stay, like a scar over a wound. Atkins imagined she couldn't have felt any other way, losing Hal as she had.

"Later, of course," Dane said. "When the boys are big enough."

Atkins felt his own eyebrows go up. It was

none of his business, but he had wondered about Dane taking her on a wagon trip when she was that far along, and now here he was, telling her how she could rough it a year or two down the line. That, and assuming that the next baby would be a boy.

"I suppose so," she said. She turned to Atkins, and it seemed for a second that an understanding passed between them. "Thanks, Tom." Then she turned to Dane and said she was going back to the house.

Dane gave a matter-of-fact nod, and when she had turned and was walking away, he said, "Well, Tom, I guess we can go ahead and take it back down. We know how it works."

Atkins said nothing. He thought that if Dane felt a little miffed, maybe he deserved some of it. He could stew on it for a while, but it most likely would not change his way of doing things. It occurred to Atkins that this was the way life now was with the Nordens, and that he and Laurel had similar ways of dealing with it.

Dane and Atkins struck the tent and rolled it up into a large bundle with the poles, ropes, and stakes inside. Then they hung it from the stable rafters, along with the other bundles of canvas. Fall roundup was long over, and now everything was put away.

Dane was not one to sit by the fire and get fat on biscuits and bacon gravy. He went back into his routine of riding out alone whenever the weather was tolerable. Atkins hung the triangle in the stable again so he could have peace of mind when he heard the bell ring at the close of day.

Sometimes he rode out with Dane. There was never much to do—just take a look here and take a look there. From time to time they had to rope an animal so they could tend to it. Range cattle were tough and didn't need much babying, but sometimes even a full-grown cow had something in her eye that needed to be dug out. When they had to rope an animal together, Atkins roped the head and Dane roped the heels. When they had the animal stretched out, Dane got down to pull a sticker from an eye or a piece of cactus from an ear. The roping came back to Atkins well enough. It was something a fellow didn't forget, just something that fell out of practice. He liked the feel of it, the old feel, when he made a good catch. And when he didn't, he just tried again. He didn't feel any urgency, no crew waiting for him to drag a calf to the fire.

In the evening, whether he had been out riding or had waited to hear the bell, life settled into its old routine. It was the time of year to mend bridles and harness, clean and oil anything made of leather. It was also the time of year to stitch up a shirt and sew up any holes on the cloth bags he used in the chuck wagon. November, the quiet time, also had some of the strongest winds of the year, whipping up at all hours and often blowing hard throughout the night. Sam took everything the same, curling and stretching and watching, greeting Atkins with a meow whenever the man came in from the cold.

Dane worked every day, so Atkins did, too, even though it was understood in ranch country that a fellow should get a day off when work was not pressing. After three weeks with no break, Atkins told Dane he thought he'd like to go to town for a day. He asked if Dane would like to go or would like him to pick up anything. Dane shook his head and said no, unless there was something he needed for the kitchen. Atkins said he would like some dried apples and canned tomatoes, so Dane told him to go ahead and get what he wanted.

Atkins rode his own horse, the stocky brown one that never gave any trouble even when he had not been ridden for months. Atkins left the ranch at midmorning, when the day was beginning to warm up, and rode into the main street of town before noon.

As he expected, Ev Mason sat on the bench in front of Chapman's store, his crutches leaning on the bench at his left. Atkins rode up to the hitching rail, dismounted, and tied up his horse. Stepping onto the sidewalk, he said hello to the motionless man in the fur cap and wool overcoat.

"Hello, Ev."

"Hello, Tom, the lone rider."

"I guess I am today."

"And how's everything out at the ranch?"

"All right, I suppose. And you?"

"No damn good." Mason turned his pale blue eyes at Atkins.

Atkins wondered if the eyes were getting dimmer. Streaks of gray were showing in the pale brown hair, and a few gray whiskers had crept into the scruffy beard. It was hard to tell about the eyes, they looked so dim against the pasty face.

"I hate to argue with you, Ev, but when you have that much energy to complain, I have to say you look as good as ever."

"I doubt that I do. But even if I do, it's no damn good."

"Ah, you're a tough old scout, Ev."

"The hell I am. I'm an old cripple with sugar in my piss, that's what I am."

"You're not that old."

"It doesn't matter. I don't have a left foot to put in the stirrup, and there's not a woman who wants a man on crutches—not unless he's a paying customer, and even then she'd probably want more."

Atkins remembered Tincher's midget from St. Louis. "There's all kinds, as far as that goes. I'd hate to suggest that a little thing like that might fix you up for a day or two."

"Don't kid yourself, Tom, and don't try to kid me. Nothing's going to fix me."

Atkins shrugged. "I can't argue with you."

"No, you can't. You don't know what it's like."

"I guess I don't. Always nice to hear the words of encouragement, though."

Mason smiled at last, as if he had gotten the conversation to the proper level. "That's what I'm here for. To give a smile and a good word to all who pass by."

Atkins patted him on the shoulder. "It's good to see you, Ev. Take care."

"You, too, Tom. Thanks for stopping."

The bell tinkled as Atkins stepped into the store and let his eyes adjust to the dim interior. It had been a while since he had patronized Chapman's business, but no great changes seemed to have taken place. The center aisle still led back to the counter, and behind that, the set of deer antlers still hung on the partition separating the store from the storeroom.

Chapman appeared behind the counter, then moved out of sight and appeared again in front of the counter. "Well, hello, Tom," he said, walking forward. "It's been a while."

"I guess it has. We stay so busy."

"Uh-huh. And what can I help you with today?" Chapman had stopped in the middle of the aisle and put on his pleasant expression—a slight tilt to the head, a relaxed look in the clear, brown eyes, and a half-smile beneath the neat mustache.

"Just a couple of things for right now," said Atkins, as if other purchases would be forthcoming.

Chapman put his palms together in front of his spreading waistcoat. "Certainly."

"I would like about ten pounds of dried apples and a dozen cans of tomatoes."

Chapman nodded. "Oh, uh-huh." As he turned, he looked back and said, "Anything else to go with that?"

"Not for now," said Atkins. He was sure Chapman had a good idea of when he had last sold flour to the NB, so a noncommittal answer was as good as an explanation.

Chapman led the way to a bin of dried apples, where he scooped out a mound of them onto a tray for the scales. "Ten pounds is quite a bit," he said. "I'll have to get a cloth bag for them." He went behind the partition and came back with a flour sack that looked as if it had been used more than once. He measured out five pounds, dumped the apples into the sack, and measured out another five pounds. Closing the neck of the sack, he turned and looked at Atkins. "Did you just ride in by yourself?"

Atkins stared at him for a moment. "Well, yes."

Chapman shook his head. "No, what I mean is, are you on horseback? If so, then I need to get something for the tomatoes."

Atkins could see that Chapman was conscious of having said something that could be misconstrued by a paying customer. "Yes," Atkins said, "I'll need something."

Chapman wrinkled his brow and said, "I think I can find a burlap bag." Within a couple of minutes he had the bag of dried apples, twelve cans of tomatoes, and an old burlap grain sack on the counter. He took out a pad and pencil, and after a moment's delay he jotted down some numbers. He looked up and gave Atkins the pleasant expression again. "And how are things out at the ranch?"

"Just fine."

"Is Mrs. Norden all right?"

"Yes, just fine."

"And the baby too, I hope."

"Oh, yes."

Chapman was still poised with the pencil. "We all felt very bad for Mrs. Norden when she lost Hal. It must have been a terrible ordeal for her."

"I believe it was."

"Such a young couple, and so happy."

"They were." Atkins felt himself tightening.

Chapman was making too much of a point of being sincere.

"We were glad Dane made the decision that he did. It seems to be the best thing for the two of them to be together."

Atkins was tempted to ask who "we" were, but instead he replied, "When two people get together, it's something they both decide."

Chapman gave him a look that implied recognition. "What I meant was, I think he was a good man for wanting to take care of her. And the baby."

Atkins moistened his lips. "I don't think you could expect any less from Dane."

Chapman went on. "And we're glad to hear that they might be expecting an addition to the family."

It seemed to Atkins that the storekeeper was making an effort to deliver a message. It meant something like, we hope these new arrangements keep Dane close to home. Thinking he had heard enough, Atkins shrugged and remarked, "Like I said, I don't think you could expect any less from Dane."

"Uh-huh." Chapman tightened up now, turning his gaze down at the figures he had jotted. "Put this on the account?"

"Sure." Atkins was glad Chapman had gone back into the refuge of being the amiable businessman.

Chapman handed him the slip to sign, and while Atkins looked it over and signed it, the storekeeper put the canned tomatoes inside the burlap sack.

"Well, here you are, Tom, and I thank you."

"Likewise."

"Give my regards to the Nordens."

"Thank you. I will. And give mine to Mrs. Chapman."

"Certainly."

On the way out of the store, Atkins waved to Ev Mason, then stepped into the street and gathered up his horse. He didn't feel like talking to Mason any more or lingering in front of Chapman's store. On another occasion he would have left the purchases in the store and gone across the street for a bath in the barbershop. But he didn't care to now. Jake, who had taken over the shop from Ralph, was not a bad sort, but Atkins had heard that Chapman was a silent partner. It didn't take much for Atkins to get his fill of Chapman, and at the moment he didn't feel like sending another two bits his way.

Atkins walked his horse down the street until he came to the Elkhorn, where he hitched the horse again. He tied the two bundles onto the back of the saddle and then, after brushing off the front of his coat, went into the saloon.

He ordered a glass of beer and tasted it. He hadn't had anything to drink for a while, and it didn't taste all that good. But it was his day off, and he had a right to a drink, so he thought he might as well take it. The second sip tasted a little better. He looked at the mirror behind the bar and got an idea of how many men were in the saloon. He counted nine, with neither Fey nor Tincher among them. That was good. He could drink the beer at his leisure.

He decided not to let Chapman's comments eat on him any longer. He was in the Elkhorn, he had a beer in front of him, and he knew Dolly was not far away.

In the parlor he asked for her, to save the other girls the trouble of coming out and putting themselves on display. After a while Dolly came out, wearing a yellow dress and a red shawl. Her blond hair was combed up into a high nest of curls, and her blue eyes sparkled.

"They told me there was a gentleman waiting for me."

"And all you found was me."

"Oh, now," she said, standing in front of him and touching her finger to his lips. "You're just the one I was looking for."

"Would you like to sit down and talk, or would you rather go to your room?"

"What would you like?"

"I think we can talk in your room, can't we?"

Her eyes sparkled as she winked. "Of course we can." She gave him her hand, and he took it as he rose from the couch. It was a warm hand. He remembered it.

In the room, she let him take off her shawl, then her dress; then her petticoat and foundation. She was not a beauty once she had her clothes off, but he liked the sensation of undressing her and of seeing a woman who was willing to be seen. He sat on the edge of the bed and let her lean into him with the softness of her perfumed breasts.

She moved her hand down to his belt, and he knew it was time for the inspection. With that interlude of business taken care of, she crawled under the covers while he finished undressing. He thought she did a nice job of letting him feel as if all of this were something they would have done without money.

"You shouldn't stay away so long," she said as they lay under the covers afterward.

"Oh, I haven't had much time off, and it takes a little more to come in by myself. I'm pretty much on my own now, you know."

"Yes, I knew that. But it's not that dangerous to come in by yourself, is it?" she teased, drumming her fingertips on his leg.

"No," he said, "not unless bad weather comes up." As he answered, a cloud moved in on his carefree moment. He hadn't thought of it in that way before, but Dolly's innocent remark made him think of Fey and Tincher. For the first time it occurred to him that the bad feelings between them and the Nordens might extend to touch him.

"And if it did," she said, "you could just stay in town for a while, couldn't you?"

"I suppose I could." He put his hand on her thigh, and he liked its softness. He could imagine doing this sort of thing more often.

"You ought to know," she went on, "that it doesn't take that much more to spend the whole night."

"That's an idea." He couldn't remember when the last time was that he spent the whole night with a woman. It had been a long while.

"I hope it's a good one."

He looked at her and smiled. "I think it is."

Atkins went back to his routine at the ranch. Sometimes he rode out with Dane, and sometimes he spent the whole day between the bunkhouse and the woodpile. From time to time he brought firewood to the back door of the little house. Hal had made it a point to keep the firewood supplied himself, but Dane didn't seem to mind letting the hired man do it.

For the next couple of weeks, Atkins saw very little of Laurel. He imagined she wasn't moving around very much, what with being as far along as she was. Once she opened the back door and asked him if he would mind bringing in an armload he was carrying. He said sure and went in.

The air inside the house was close and stale, and the housekeeping had not been kept up. Atkins remembered how neat the place had been when she was married to Hal, and he attributed the difference to her current condition. She thanked him without looking straight at him, and he was glad to be outside once again in the cold, fresh air.

November gave way to December. It occurred to Atkins that Hal had been dead for almost a year. A great deal had changed in the lives of Dane and Laurel, and the baby was a year old now, but in other ways the world seemed to go on the same way. A man lived, a man died, and outside his small circle of family and friends, the world did not take much trouble to see if it had done right by him. Atkins thought it might not be the responsibility of the world out there; it should be, but maybe it wasn't accepted. It ought to be someone's lookout, he thought, but he was a fine one to think he could do anything to make it happen.

Dane still came and went as always. Atkins could not help harboring the thought that Dane liked getting out of the house where a lumbering pregnant woman moved among heaps of undone work. Not that Dane ever avoided work—he just liked to choose his jobs when he could. And so he came and went, ringing the bell at the close of day.

On the night of December 6, while Atkins sat in front of the sheet-iron stove cleaning a pair of boots and trading glances with Sam, Dane came bursting into the bunkhouse.

"I need your help, Tom. Laurel's time has come."

Atkins was on his feet in an instant. "Shall I hitch up the wagon?" He knew Dane had been keeping horses in the stable at night for the last week.

Dane stopped on his way out of the room. "Well, I don't know."

Atkins held out his hand in a gesture of calmness. "Stop and think, Dane. You've got Laurel, and you've got the baby. You need a pile of blankets and a valise of clothes."

"She's got all that stuff ready."

"Well, you need to get it all to the front door, and I'll help you load her into the wagon. Now, do you want me to go along? I can drive if you want me to."

"Um, I assumed I would drive the wagon. You can go along if you want, though."

"All right. I'll saddle a horse to tie to the back of the wagon, so I can have something to ride back."

Dane stalled. "Well, I could do some of that—"

"Dane, I'll do it. You get your wife to the front door, and you get the baby bundled up. I'll do the rest."

As Atkins went to hitch up the horses, he let out a long breath. What the hell was it about a man like Dane, he thought, who didn't have enough fear when he should, but who couldn't deal with a woman having a baby?

Atkins rode back late that same night. He could have spent the night with Dane and Laurel at Ralph and Susie's house, but he was irked at Dane for not having brought Laurel in sooner. He stayed long enough for the doctor to get there and assure everyone that things were all right. At about eleven that night, Laurel had a second baby in her arms. They named him Hal.

Chapter Twelve

Atkins poked the point of the iron gambrel through the hind shanks of the steer, then signaled for Dane to pull the slack out of the rope. Dane hauled down on the rope that came out of the block and tackle, and the other end of the rope tightened. The hind legs of the steer, with the skinned shanks showing white and pink, stiffened with the tension of the rope and gambrel. Sure that the cross-iron was lodged firm, Atkins went to help Dane hoist the steer off the stable floor.

Dane had picked out a nice one, a two-year-old with a brand that neither Dane nor Atkins recognized. The steer had been grazing with a bunch of NB stock, so Dane and Atkins had brought them in as a group at the end of the day.

A single shot from Dane's revolver lifted all four feet off the ground and dumped the steer on its side. Now they could skin it and get it cleaned out, a job that would go a little slower by lantern light, and the carcass would cool just fine overnight.

"I'll run these other cattle back out a ways before I put away the horses," Dane said.

Atkins said all right. By the time Dane came back, unsaddled and put away the two horses they had just ridden, and fed the half-dozen horses he kept in the corral, Atkins had the steer skinned down to the front quarters. Dane said he was going to check in on Laurel and would be back in a few minutes.

Once Atkins had finished the skinning, he did not take long to open up the abdomen and haul out the entrails. He knew to save the heart for Laurel, but everything else would go to the coyotes and magpies—except the liver, which would keep Sam happy for over a week.

Back in the bunkhouse, Atkins lit a lantern and washed up, scrubbing the dried blood off his knuckles, wrists, and forearms. He had another day's work done, and a good piece of beef was hanging in the stable. Tomorrow he and Dane would quarter it, put a front quarter in each house, and leave the hind quarters wrapped in canvas in the toolroom. The meat would keep for a long time in this weather.

John D. Nesbitt

Atkins built up a fire in the cookstove, then sliced some bacon for supper. He would be glad to have fresh beef, and he imagined Laurel would be, too. Dane, who did not scruple to kill a range beef, had still taken a week of reminders to bring one in.

Time went on, Atkins thought. It was the end of January. His birthday had come and gone, and February was around the corner. Hal had been dead for well over a year now. Atkins had been aware of it since shortly after the baby was born, but now with the passing of his birthday, and his fortieth at that, his sense of time moving on had sharpened.

He wondered if, after all, anyone was going to do anything about Hal's death. Atkins had given up long ago on someone outside the family going to any more bother, and now he began to wonder if Dane would be able to do anything in the way of bringing about justice. He still had faith in Dane for being strong, solid, and capable. And he was sure Dane had not forgotten about it. He just wondered if, at this late date, there was anything Dane could do.

The next day, a cold wind blew out of the north and whistled around the buildings at the ranch. Atkins hustled to bring in firewood, then waited to hear from Dane. At midmorning the two of them quartered the beef and took care of it as planned. Dane said he did not expect to ride

216

out that day, so Atkins spent the afternoon baking an apple pie.

He built up the fire in the stove, then set the dried apples in water to simmer as he rolled out the dough. When the apples were soft he mixed in the sugar, the cinnamon, and a couple of spoonfuls of flour. The fragrance rose from the mixture, and the mess thickened up well. He scraped it into the pie shell, then laid on the top crust, pinched it down, and cut airholes.

When Dane was feeding the horses at sundown, Atkins told him he thought he might bring over a pie after supper if they didn't have any other engagements. Dane said he thought the calendar was open. Later that evening, Atkins wrapped the pie in a flour sack and carried it, still warm from sitting on the shelf above the stove, to the little house.

The inside of the house had returned to a semblance of neatness. The dishes were all put away, the hats and coats hung on their pegs, and the floor was picked up. Baby Dane was sitting up in his mother's lap, and baby Hal lay gurgling in a wicker bassinet in front of the stove. The kitchen table had been cleared, so Atkins set down the pie.

As he took off his hat and shrugged out of his coat, he took a look at Laurel. Although she had shed the look of heaviness she had carried earlier, she did not look young and happy any more.

She still had a closed-over appearance, as if she had drawn a curtain over whatever had made her happy before and whatever had taken the happiness away. Her eyes sparkled as she dandled the baby in her lap, but the joy did not pervade her whole presence. Atkins recalled the night he had ridden into town with her and baby Dane in the back of the wagon. She had not complained much, just let out a sound once in a while that was midway between a sigh and a cry. He had given her a hand at those times, a gloved hand like her own, to hold until the pain let up.

"It's very nice of you, Tom," she said. "I should have made a pie by now, but with two of the little ones I'm just learning how to keep up."

Atkins looked from the larger baby to the smaller one. He imagined it kept her busy, and he felt a twinge of guilt for having so much leisure to himself. He brushed away that feeling and said, "Glad to be able to." He took a chair and sat back from the table, so as not to sit right between Dane and Laurel.

"This one's walking now," she said, "and he gets heavier every day." She turned the infant around and set him on the floor. "Here. Go to Dad."

Dane turned in his chair and held out his hands. The baby took a step, took another, then teetered and began to fall to his right. Atkins leaned forward and caught him, then gave him a hand to grab and steered him toward Dane.

"Not jealous, is he?" Atkins asked, motioning with his head toward the bassinet.

"Oh, no," Laurel said. "He just loves his little brother. Thank God he's not any bigger, or he'd be dragging him around like a puppy."

Atkins laughed and looked at Dane, who had a smile on his face as he held the hands of his little namesake. "I suppose that's next, I guess— huh, Dane? Get a puppy for these little boys?"

Dane nodded. "I suppose. No hurry, though. These tykes are pretty small yet."

Atkins looked at Laurel, who was unwrapping the pie.

She looked back and said, "They'll grow up in no time. As soon as little Dane is old enough to talk, he'll be wanting a puppy. I know little boys." She looked at Dane the elder.

He gave a clever smile. "He needs to know what one is before he knows what he's missing. Maybe we just won't take 'im to town. Leave him here with Tom."

Atkins laughed again. "Then he'll be pesterin' you for a cat."

"Yeah, well, maybe so. But there's still no hurry. He can't even say 'dog' yet. He can barely say 'mama.' "

Laurel nodded. "He's not much of a talker yet. But he'll catch up. That's the way my brother

219

Jimmy was. Once he started talking, he never shut up. Not to this day."

Not knowing Jimmy, Atkins connected the comment with someone he did know—a cow-puncher with a rough face and a dull eye. "Some people are like that," he said.

Dane shifted in his chair and said nothing. Atkins wondered if he was trying to prove it didn't apply to him or if he didn't even pay any attention to the small talk.

The wind let up the next day. Atkins cut firewood in the morning and got his day organized so he could ride out with Dane in the afternoon. When they rode out of the ranch, the day had warmed up to above freezing and the sun was shining.

They went through the hills to the north, where the country opened up into wide plains. The landscape lay pale in its winter colors of tan and gray. Patches of old snow lay here and there, dirty snow with dust blown into it. Atkins, feeling the sun warm on his back and on his horse's neck, knew the warmth of such a day was fragile at best. Antelope and cattle would be grazing out in the open, but it was chilly enough that a cow-puncher would like to find a south-facing bluff and take in the reflected warmth for a while.

Dane, who had no doubt smoked many a cig-arette in the lee of a bluff or cutbank, was on the move today. He told Atkins they would ride out

in two big circles—Atkins to the east and Dane
to the west, and meet back at this spot in about
two hours. Atkins looked at the sun and said all
right.

He looked back once and saw Dane angling
off to the northwest. He saw the mountains to
the west, dark patches interspersed with white.
Then he looked back around to the north and
east, to pay attention to his own ride.

Cattle were sparse where he rode. Twice he
saw large grazed-off areas where they had held
the roundup herd. He rode past the two burned-
out camps, to fix in his mind once again their
exact location. Sometimes when he rode over the
country he could fancy that it was new, but at
times like this he had no such illusion. It was all
a big pasture, worn here and there with marks
of man and his beasts. Atkins could see where he
had changed the earth with his shovel and mattock. The alteration was on a smaller scale than
the changes made by a wheat farmer or a ditch
crew, but it was there.

Atkins rode around to the south, still on his
big circle, and curved back to the west. At his
farthest point south he saw two coyotes, and a
little while after that he saw a band of five antelope. He still saw few cattle.

The sun was slipping in the southwest when
he came to the flat where he had agreed to meet
Dane. The land spread out level for about a mile

221

in all four directions. Off to the west it fell away before rising again farther off. Atkins decided to ride over to the edge where he could keep an eye out for Dane.

He saw a lone rider down in the low spot, headed this way. It looked like Dane. Atkins waited, wondering if Dane would look up. Then he saw two riders angling in from the northwest. He felt a lurch in his stomach as he registered the impression of two men on dark horses.

Atkins put his horse into a lope. The other riders, Dane by himself as well as the pair, would catch the motion unless they were very intent on one another. Even at that, they would hear hoofbeats before long.

When Atkins had ridden to within half a mile, Dane looked up and stopped his horse. The other two riders had dipped out of sight, but Atkins assumed they had seen him and had realized he had seen them. Atkins slowed his horse to a walk and came up alongside Dane.

"What's your hurry?"

Atkins motioned with his head, then spoke in a low voice. "Two riders."

Dane raised his eyebrows and looked off to his left. "Let 'em come."

Atkins turned his horse around and stopped next to Dane, both of them looking north. After a few minutes, two riders loomed up out of the prairie on dark horses. It was Fey and Tincher, just as he had thought.

"Come on, you sons of bitches," Dane said in a low voice.

Fey and Tincher rode forward. Atkins noticed that they both carried rifles tucked away in scabbards. They were also both wearing gloves, which meant they weren't likely to pull a six-gun without notice. Atkins looked over at Dane and saw that he was wearing gloves also. Just as well, he thought.

When the other two riders had come within twenty yards, Dane spoke. "Did you find who you were lookin' for?"

Fey put both gloved hands on the saddle horn. "What makes you think we were lookin' for someone?"

"Just a guess."

Fey stretched his face. "There's lots of guesses to be made. Who knows if any of 'em would be right." He glanced at Atkins and then turned his brown eyes back on Dane.

Atkins took the opportunity to observe Fey. He had never thought of the man as much of a cowpuncher, what with his showy silver spurs and his pushy manner. Fey had hired gun written all over him. Atkins then looked across at Tincher, who was more of a cowpuncher but did not shed the general demeanor of a saddle tramp. He had let his beard grow to cover some of his rough face, but he had not improved his appearance. As usual, Tincher moved his head to follow the conversation.

"Who knows," Dane mimicked. "But if you're not lookin' for someone, you found us anyway."

"Wouldn't have been polite not to say hello." Then, before anyone could answer, Fey added, "And besides, we thought we'd drop a friendly word."

"Is that right? About what?" Dane's face was hard.

Fey showed his teeth. "Nothin' new, really. Just the same old story of beef disappearing."

Atkins could see Dane's jaw muscles tighten. "What's that supposed to mean?"

"You ought to know. You claim that you come up short. Well, some of the Argentine count seems low."

Dane seemed to relax. "And you think we had anything to do with that?"

"Didn't say that. But if you're wonderin' what we're doin' out here, you can imagine we're doin' the same as you—lookin' out for our brand."

Atkins looked at Tincher and then back at Fey. He doubted that they had been keeping a very close eye on cattle, or they would have mentioned the beef that got butchered two days earlier. He imagined Dane was thinking along the same lines, given the way he had tensed up and then relaxed. He saw Dane lick his lips and give Fey a hard look.

"You'd be pretty harmless if that was all you were up to."

Fey narrowed his eyes. "What's that supposed to mean?"

"Just what I said. If you were just out lookin' for cattle that no one laid a hand on, you wouldn't be much trouble."

Fey's mouth was open now, but his teeth did not show. He had his upper lip and bristly mustache pulled tight over his teeth. "Why don't you come out and say what you mean?"

"You know what I mean. I told you before. I think you've been out on the range before when you weren't just lookin' for cattle." Dane paused for a couple of seconds and went on. "I don't think my brother died by accident. You already knew what I thought, and you don't have to pretend you didn't."

Fey lifted his lip now and showed his teeth. "You need to be careful about what you say, Norden."

"I'm saying it good and clear, in front of two other men. You're a coward, Fey. If you ever want to have it out, man-to-man, just come forward. Don't come sneakin' around. Just you and me"—Dane pointed to Fey and then to himself—"man-to-man, face-to-face."

Atkins was impressed with Fey's composure.

Here was a man who had been slapped in the face and was now called a coward, showing neither resentment nor fear.

"I'm gonna let you cool down, Norden, and not get yourself into much trouble shootin' off your mouth. But take my word for it. When you see me, it'll be face-to-face."

Atkins looked at Fey and recalled a comment he had made the day Dane slapped him. He had told Dane to watch his back. Now he was saying the opposite, in words that Atkins took as false.

"Good," said Dane, motioning with his head. "And you can leave your egg-suckin' pal out of it."

Atkins saw Tincher stiffen and Fey clench his teeth. Tincher must have been under strict orders not to say anything, as he just looked at Fey and waited for him to talk.

"Don't worry about that. You can even bring your nursemaid here along. It won't make a difference."

Now Tincher spoke. "Dane, I never done anything to you or your brother either one. But I don't owe you nothin', and even less after today."

Atkins wished Dane would let it go, but he didn't.

"Go to hell, Mike. I told you that before, and I'm tellin' you again." He looked at Fey. "Both of you. You'd both be better off if you stayed away from me, but I'll take on either of you, one-on-one."

Fey looked at Tincher. "I think everyone's said enough for today." Then he turned back to look at Atkins. "How about you, Dolly? Did you want to say something?"

Atkins flinched but shook his head.

Fey showed his teeth. "You might be the smartest one of the bunch, but that don't say much." He looked at Tincher, motioned with his head, and dug a spur into the dark horse.

"Cowardly sons of bitches," Dane said as they rode away. "I don't think either of 'em has it in him."

"Not face-to-face," said Atkins. "And not by themselves. But I wouldn't count 'em out." He shook his head. "They're the type that if you meet 'em at the front gate, they'll go around back."

"They'd better be good at it," Dane said. "I've been waitin' for 'em a long time, and they won't catch me nappin'." He took off his gloves and pulled the makin's from a vest pocket inside his coat.

Atkins watched as Dane built his cigarette with steady hands. Still scowling, Dane put the cigarette in his mouth, popped a match, and lit the smoke. He held the dead match for a while, as was his habit, to let it go cold before he tossed it on the ground. As he blew away a second cloud of smoke, he looked at Atkins and shook his head.

"They don't have it in 'em," he said.

Atkins shrugged. "Maybe they know that."

What Fey and Tincher had in them, and what they knew, gave Atkins something to speculate about for the next few days. He was convinced Fey had plenty in him, and what he lacked in courage he made up for in brazenness and malice. It also seemed that he went out of his way to find out personal details about a man so he could get in a dig when it wasn't expected. He had to have gone to a little trouble to find out who Atkins's girl of preference was. Using her name was a safe insult for him to make toward Atkins as well as the girl. Fey was good at nasty insinuations. Atkins could count three women he had made remarks about, but he picked his topics well enough that he got slapped for only one of them.

What Tincher had in him made for less interesting speculation. Atkins figured him for more courage and less malice, but not strong enough principles to keep him from playing along. Twice now, Tincher had gone to the trouble of protesting his innocence in Hal's death. Atkins took that to mean he hadn't leveled the blow himself. But he had it in him to be a second party, and he would probably have less reluctance to make a move on Dane than on Hal, especially, as he had said, after this last run-in.

Dane, meanwhile, gave no indication of fearing what Fey and Tincher had in them. He came and went as before, sometimes with Atkins and sometimes on his own. Atkins feared for him, but at the same time he had confidence in him. Dane was solid. He had nerve, and he wasn't going to let someone pick him off like a rabbit.

Then, on the seventh of February, Atkins's confidence began to waver. Dane had ridden out by himself in the afternoon, and sundown slipped by without the sound of the triangle. After dark, Atkins put on his coat and hat and went to count the horses in the corral. Dane had been keeping six there, and Atkins counted only five. They hadn't been fed. That meant that Dane hadn't come in and just forgotten to ring the bell. Atkins felt the worry start to gnaw at him with more force. His heart was beating faster, and his stomach was tight.

He wondered if he should go knock on the door of the little house. He didn't want to worry Laurel, he tried to tell himself, but he knew she would already be worried plenty. He was sure she had been worried every day since Hal died, and he saw no reason to make her sit and fret by herself until it got the best of her and sent her to knock on the door of the bunkhouse once again.

She opened the door before he was finished

knocking. "Tom! Has something happened to Dane?"

"I don't know, but I haven't seen any sign of him."

She shook her head. "I knew it. I knew something was going to happen. I told him we should leave, but he would never listen. And now—"

"Let's try to stay calm, Laurel. To begin with, we don't know if anything has happened. He may have had his horse go lame, or leave him on foot. Maybe he—"

"I know, I know. He said the same things when Hal didn't come home. But I knew. I could feel it."

Atkins did not have to ask if she felt it again. He could tell. "Well, if something has happened, we'd better find out as soon as we can, and then decide what we're going to do about it."

Laurel had a hard, angry look on her face. "What we're going to do? Well, it shouldn't take too long to decide that. I've got two little baby boys to take care of. I'm not going to sit around here and wait for—"

"All right, all right. I know we've got to do something, and not waste time. I hate to leave you here by yourself, but I think I'd better go out and see if I can find anything."

Atkins went back to the bunkhouse, rolled up a pair of blankets to tie onto the back of the saddle, and put his six-gun and holster on his belt.

Then he went to the stable, where he saddled a horse by lantern light. In the last few evenings he had noticed the moon was in its waxing phase, getting a little fuller each evening and rising farther to the east. Now it was between a half-moon and a three-quarter-moon, which would have given him good moonlight to travel by, except that a cloud cover had moved in from the west and cast a murky pall on the night.

He rode out north, in the direction he thought Dane had gone in the afternoon. It was a big country, with only a few yards of it to be seen at a time. It gave him a feeling of hopelessness to think of how little ground he was actually covering. He imagined it was the way Dane had felt when he went out looking for his brother—a sinking sense of futility that played off against a bedrock feeling of having to give it a try.

It was a quiet night, so he took some hope in the possibility that he might hear something or that his horse might nicker to Dane's. It was a good hope, but it came to nothing. He rode across the dark landscape for more than three hours, finally giving it up for a loss and arriving back at the ranch at about eleven.

Laurel was sitting up, rocking baby Hal in front of the kitchen stove. The look on her face conveyed an understanding as Atkins shook his head.

"Nothing at all," he said.

"Well, we might as well try to get some sleep. I made you a bed on the floor."

Morning brought a gray, empty feeling. Atkins knew that sooner or later the day was going to confirm his fears. He had no hope, only dread.

After breakfast, while the new day was still in the first hour of overcast gray, he went to the stable. There stood a large sorrel horse with Dane's saddle on it. Atkins felt as if someone had just kicked him in the stomach. Speaking in a gentle voice, he eased up to the horse and took its reins. He looked over the animal for nicks and wounds; he inspected the saddle for drops of blood. All he could determine was that the horse had come in by itself.

Saddling a fresh horse, Atkins rode back out to the north. A light, thin snow was starting to fall, but he could see for nearly a mile. He rode a pattern of overlapping circles, then a zigzag, then the circles again. Late in the morning he found what he had sensed as inevitable.

Dane was lying facedown with his arms spread out. His hat lay a few yards away, dusted with a scattering of small snowflakes. His tan canvas coat also bore an undisturbed sprinkling of snow that had fallen after the body went still. As Atkins recognized the little hole in the middle of the garment, he felt the cold, detached, numb feeling all over again. Dane Norden, as brave a man as he had known, lay dead from a bullet in the back.

Atkins knelt by him on the cold, wintry plain. "I'm sorry, Dane," he said out loud. "I'm sorry." And in that moment he forgave Dane for all his stubbornness and for ever slighting Laurel.

Chapter Thirteen

Atkins leveled the coals with his iron poker, then put in three pieces of firewood. Still with the poker, he closed the front door of the cookstove and lifted the latch into place. He sat down on a chair and went back to thinking about how things stood at the NB. He knew he was in too deep in this whole mess to just quit and ride away. At the very least, he had to get Laurel and the boys to town. He had left her for a few hours so she could heat bathwater, bathe herself and the little ones, and pack the things she wanted to take to town. She said she wanted to get off this forsaken ranch and into the house in town. Then she could decide what she was going to do next.

Atkins figured he could do the same, once he got them to town. At spare moments, he thought he could ride back down to Pueblo and stay with Diego's people for a while. It seemed like a pleasant idea, but he knew he couldn't do it—not right away, at least. He couldn't just walk away from things that weren't resolved, especially the injustice of Dane's death. He felt he had to stick it out for a while longer, even if he couldn't do anything conclusive himself. After bringing Dane into town in the wagon, he had gotten the sheriff to ride out right away and look at the scene of the murder. To his credit, the sheriff had done that and some questioning as well. Then he had come by to tell Laurel and Atkins what he had determined.

He said he had found no telling evidence at the scene of the killing, and Fey and Tincher had a solid story of having been at the Argentine Ranch for several days straight.

Atkins said of course Cobarde would have an alibi for them, since he was the one who wanted to push out the Nordens to begin with.

The sheriff said that might all be true, but he needed more evidence. He had no doubt that murder had been committed, but he needed more to go on if he thought he was going to arrest somebody.

Back in the bunkhouse now, Atkins ruminated on it. He couldn't believe that someone could get away with one murder and probably two, yet it looked as if that might happen. For all that he

John D. Nesbitt

had hoped someone might be able to do something about Hal's death, no one had. He could imagine how the same thing could happen now. No one could do anything without more proof, and where was the proof going to come from? Atkins felt powerless. At least before, he could have confidence in Dane's capability, but now he had nothing.

From where he sat, he opened the door of the cookstove and saw that the logs had caught fire and were blazing away. He closed the door again, set the poker aside, and set a skillet on top of the stove. After spooning in a dab of bacon grease, he held his left hand, palm down, next to the skillet. Heat was rising through the iron stovetop. That was good. At least a man could eat.

With Sam's eyes on him, he cut two steaks from the front quarter of beef. He trimmed off some scraps of fat and tossed them to Sam, saw that the bacon grease had melted, and laid the meat in the pan. As he poked at the steaks with his long-handled fork, he thought it was all fine and good to be snug in the NB bunkhouse with grub on the way, but he was going to have to do something. He didn't know what it would be, but if he didn't do anything, it might come down to self-defense. The thought chilled him. If they could get to Dane that easily, what chance did he have? He poked again at the steaks. If he had any advantage at all, it would be in not commit-

236

ting Dane's error. He would allow himself to have fear.

After his noon dinner, Atkins hitched up the wagon and pulled it close to the door of the house. Laurel had the boys and bundles ready. She stayed inside the doorway and handed the lighter items to Atkins, who stowed them in the wagon. The heavier things, such as the boxes of groceries and the half-quarter of beef, he went in and fetched himself. He got things well stacked in the wagon, making something of a nest for the two little boys and leaving a space for Laurel next to them. When he asked her if she had anything for padding to lie or sit on, she brought Dane's bedroll. Atkins laid it out, and the wagon was ready. He went back to the door of the house.

Laurel handed the baby in the bassinet to Atkins. Then with a heave she lifted little Dane onto her hip. She paused before pulling the door closed.

"I don't know when I'll be back to get the rest," she said. "Who knows if someone will come and rummage through it."

"I think they've done as much damage as they wanted," Atkins said, but he did not feel convinced by his own words.

Laurel gave him a straight look with her blue-gray eyes. She wore a dark wool cap, and her face was framed by her dark hair. Despite her pale complexion, she was a picture of firmness as she

John D. Nesbitt

spoke. "They won't be satisfied until they have the whole ranch. And I won't be satisfied until someone pays for what they've done." She closed the door. "If there was a way that a woman could take a gun and go after them, I'd think hard about doing it, but I know it can't be done."

"You're right," Atkins said. His words sounded hollow and he knew he should say more, but he didn't have anything else to offer. He carried the bassinet to the wagon, set it in, then took little Dane and swung him up and over the sideboards. After helping Laurel climb in, he took his place on the wagon seat and started the drive into town.

From time to time he looked in back to see how everyone was riding. It was a tolerable day for the trip, cold but not windy, with the sun breaking through the clouds in the early part of the afternoon. A little more snow had fallen in the two days since he found Dane, but the landscape did not look much different. The bleak colors of winter prevailed, brightened here and there by the fugitive sunlight falling on patches of snow.

Dusk was drawing in by the time he got everything unloaded and into Ralph and Susie's house. Atkins didn't like the idea of driving back to the ranch alone that evening, so he took Laurel's suggestion and put up the horses in the little stable out back. He imagined someone might

238

have an unkind word about his staying in the house with the widow while Dane was still at the undertaker's, but that seemed like a small matter at the moment.

Laurel had packed a good supply of groceries from her kitchen at the ranch, so the house smelled of cooking food when Atkins came in through the back door. Warmth from the cookstove had cut the chill in the air, and the light from the kitchen spread into the front room. Atkins saw Dane's bedroll on the floor with two folded blankets stacked on top of it. That would be fine, he thought, for as much as he was likely to sleep. He did feel that his presence was useful, though, so he thought it was a good idea to stay in town and then go back to the ranch after the funeral tomorrow afternoon.

In the morning he tended to the horses and brought in a scuttle of coal. Laurel had fixed gravy and biscuits along with a pot of coffee, so the two of them sat down to breakfast. Laurel said very little, and Atkins felt they didn't have much to talk about except the details of here and now. He offered to go back out to the ranch for a few days and look after things until she decided what she was going to do.

She said she appreciated it. She said she needed to get through today first, and then she could think about what came next.

After breakfast, Atkins decided he would go

to the barbershop. He had not brought along a change of clothes, but a shave and a bath would make him feel all right about paying his respects to Dane. He took leave of Laurel and walked downtown.

Chapman must have been watching from the store. Atkins had barely taken a seat to wait for his shave when Chapman came across the street, bareheaded, and entered the barbershop. He stood inside the closed door, a couple of feet away from Atkins's knee.

"Tom," he said, in an earnest tone, "I can't tell you how bad we feel about what has happened."

Atkins lifted a cold look his way. "Appreciate your mentionin' it."

Chapman gave a sigh. "And how is Mrs. Norden? Is she holding up?"

"She's all right, considering what she's been through."

"It's the worst imaginable. And with two little babies." Chapman had on his soft look, with his brown eyes full of concern. "Are they all staying here in town?"

"Yes, they are."

"Well, if they need anything at all, let me know. I'll send it right over."

"I'll do that."

"And yourself, Tom?"

Atkins lifted his eyebrows. "What about me?"

"Are you staying at the ranch all by yourself? That is, after today?"

Atkins resented what might be an intimation about where he had spent the night, and at the same time his pride rose within him at the suggestion that he shouldn't stay alone. "Don't worry about me, Al. I might wear an apron, but I'm not gelded."

"But being out there by yourself, after what's happened?"

"I'm not a baby, Al. I sleep with one eye open." He looked at Chapman, broad and complacent, and he felt contempt. "It's not something that comes naturally, but I've learned to. Unlike some people, I have to close my left eye to aim a rifle."

"Don't take me wrong, now, Tom."

"Don't worry about it."

Chapman nodded, having fallen back into his obsequious manner. "Please give our sympathy to Mrs. Norden. Our kindest regards."

Now Atkins understood Chapman's main purpose in the visit. It was his way of saying he wouldn't attend the funeral. Well, Atkins didn't expect him to. "I'll do that," he said.

When Atkins had finished with his shave and his bath, he stood inside the barbershop door and looked out onto the street. Across the way, Ev Mason had taken his usual spot on the bench in front of Chapman's mercantile. Behind him, the store windows reflected the pale sunlight and gray sky. Despite Chapman's apparent speaking for himself and his wife, Atkins felt as if he needed to give her a chance to say something. He wondered if Mrs. Chapman was inside the store, but he didn't feel like jousting with Ev Mason in order to find out.

The time came for the funeral. Because of the babies, Laurel had decided to have the services in the undertaker's parlor and then a brief visit to the cemetery for the burial. Feeling cold and tight and empty, Atkins helped her as she got ready to leave the house. She wrapped little Dane in a blanket and handed him to Atkins. Then she wrapped little Hal and cradled him in her arms. Atkins opened the door, let her walk through, and then closed it.

He did not expect many people to show up, what with it being the middle of the week and on such short notice. In the case of a man like Dane, who did not go out of his way to make friends, it would not pain many people to have something else to do—especially if they, too, felt some guilt about nobody doing much about the killing.

Atkins walked along the board sidewalk, carrying little Dane and trying to keep an eye out for Laurel's path as she walked. Just before they reached the undertaker's parlor, he looked up and saw Mrs. Chapman, her white face and blond hair recognizable above a dark overcoat.

She must have been waiting somewhere, feigning interest in one of the shops, until the moment arrived. Of a sudden she appeared in front of him, slowing but not stopping. She met his gaze as they passed one another, shoulder to shoulder on the sidewalk. Her blue eyes, which once had carried a spark of adventure, showed a sadness that she could not speak. Atkins understood it was the best she could do. She could not have gone into the parlor, he knew that, but with her wordless glance she had done what she could. She showed she had some feeling about what had happened to Dane.

Atkins arrived at the ranch at dusk. Seeing a faint glow of light in the bunkhouse window, he left the wagon in front of the stable and walked over for a look. Making as little noise as possible on the dry ground and patchy snow, he drew up to the window and looked inside. Sitting in front of the sheet-iron stove, with Sam in his lap, was Diego.

Atkins went inside. As soon as he saw Diego's face, he knew the young man had heard the news. Diego said the murder had been in the Colorado papers. A friend of his family, knowing he had worked in Wyoming, showed him the newspaper. He came right away on the train to Wheatland, then rented a horse. After some hesitation he asked when the funeral would be, and Atkins told him the burial had already taken place.

"And his wife? Did she have the other baby?"

"Yes, she did. They're all in town. I just got back with the wagon."

Diego helped him put away the wagon and horses. Then they went back into the bunkhouse, where Atkins began fixing the evening meal.

Diego said once again how terrible it was that someone could get killed and no one would do anything. "I feel I should do something," he said.

"I feel the same way, but I don't think there's much either of us can do."

"And his wife? What will she do?"

"Oh, I think she'll have to sell the ranch. Now that both the boys have gotten killed over it, or at least that's the way it looks, I think she just wants to be rid of it."

"And you, Tom?"

Atkins shrugged. "There's always work somewhere. But I don't think there'll be any here, for you or me, come springtime."

Diego's eyes were still moist. "But it's just not right. They treat me so good, I can't just leave the ranch to go to hell."

Atkins gave a small shake to his head. He didn't want to come right out and say it, but he knew that if Diego stayed around he stood a chance of getting hurt. Diego was loyal to the boys, but it was not in his nature to fight for blood. Atkins picked his words. "It's not a matter of leaving it," he said. "There just won't be anything to come back to."

Tears started in Diego's eyes as he shook his head. "Both of them. So young, so strong. And making a ranch for their family."

"I know. But they're gone. We can't change that. And the NB ranch won't be around for long, either."

They talked on, along the same lines, as Atkins finished frying the beef and potatoes. By the time they sat down to eat, he had convinced Diego that there wouldn't be any work to come back to and there wasn't anything either of them could do to change that.

Diego said he would go back in the morning but he wanted to go to the cemetery first. Atkins said he would ride into town with him.

The next morning, they set out for town. They made the ride without incident, arriving shortly before noon. Atkins went with Diego as he paid his respects at the cemetery and gave his condolences to Laurel. Then Diego rode south, while Atkins headed west back to the ranch.

Clouds were building in the west. For the past three days it looked as if it was going to snow, and now it looked even more so. Atkins was glad Laurel and the boys were safe in town. He hoped Diego got back to the train all right and didn't get caught in bad weather. It was just as well he

245

didn't stay around very long. He could have gotten hurt. Atkins looked around him as he rode. What used to seem like an innocent country looked threatening now. He remembered how he used to feel safe and alone under God's eye; now it seemed a lone rider was at risk. Flat as the country looked, it held too many places for surprises.

Back at the ranch, Atkins put his horse away and went to the bunkhouse. He had a couple of hours to while away before he did the evening chores. He was too keyed up to take a nap, but he could do with a little time to think things out. A ride by himself was often good for that, but the trip back from town had been one long lookout, and he hadn't cleared his mind of much of anything.

He built a fire in the sheet-iron stove, then sat on a chair in front of it. Alone now in his familiar surroundings, he felt an awareness sink in. Everyone else was gone. There was no one in the little house, no one out riding who would come in later. He was on his own, with nothing more definite on his mind than to look after things. He had gotten Laurel out of harm's way, and now he was looking out for her interests. That idea made him feel useful, until his thoughts looped back. Laurel hadn't really been in danger before. He knew that at the time. But if he got her to a place where she felt safer, it amounted to the same thing. But the danger itself he hadn't felt. He hadn't been afraid at all when he drove her and the boys to town. Now that he thought of it, why should he? They were as good as a shield. He winced at the idea. It gave him a little shame to think in those terms, but it was probably true. And now it wasn't working that way. He was on his own.

The problem was, he didn't have a plan. That was what was wrong. He knew he should do something, but he didn't know what. No, even that wasn't right. Deep down, he knew what he should do, and that was to go after Fey. But he didn't know how to go about it. That was his problem. He didn't have a plan for that.

Sitting here like a duck, that was what he was doing. He wondered if Fey would come after him. What motivation would Fey have? Maybe some. Maybe not enough. Atkins had been there when Dane slapped him, again when Dane told him he knew Hal's death was no accident, and again when Dane called him a coward and gave him an open challenge. Atkins wondered if that was enough to make Fey come after him. He shook his head. He was sure Fey had killed Dane. The man had gotten even, saving face in his own way, while he did a piece of work for Cobarde. He should be satisfied with that.

Still, Atkins was the one witness to that last encounter between Dane and Fey. Now that

Dane had been shot in the back, that flare-up could easily be shown as the provocation. Fey might see him as a potential danger just because he was there.

So what? he told himself. He had stayed out of it, showed no willingness to take part. He had kept his mouth shut.

Or had he? He thought back to the scene with Chapman in the barbershop. He hadn't kept his mouth shut. He had as much as said, "I'm ready. Let 'em come. I know who they are." As he thought of it, he had a sinking feeling. Chapman had no love for Atkins, perhaps even less so after his remarks about how two people chanced to get together and about what a person could expect from Dane when it came to women. Chapman would have known Atkins was privy to the affair, and he probably begrudged him for being a go-between, whether he had proof or not.

Everybody knew everything. That was the trouble. Fey knew about Mrs. Chapman, and he knew about Dolly. Fey and Chapman would have talked, especially since Chapman had sidled up to the Argentine Ranch. Chapman probably knew about Dane and Atkins and the parlor girls, and he probably had to bite his tongue to keep from giving it away. No, he would not care what happened to Atkins any more than he cared about Dane. One man had done him wrong, and the other had rubbed it in—that was how Chapman would see it.

Atkins realized that regardless of whether Chapman mentioned something to Fey or not, he had been careless. He had said too much. Now he was back here alone, left to brood on his own mistakes. One big one was talking too much. Sure, he was defending his pride, but had he been borrowing courage, faced only with Chapman, in the safety of a barbershop? He could see it was an error now. So was coming back here by himself. If anyone had the slightest inclination to make a move on him, he could do it. Sleeping with one eye open—that was a brave thing to say, but it was a big country out there, and he didn't have eyes in the back of his head. Neither did Dane—or Hal, either.

He needed a plan, that was what he had to focus on. He had thought that if he just stayed out of things, everyone would leave him alone. He couldn't bet on that. He remembered Fey taunting him when he called him Dolly. Atkins hadn't said anything, just brushed it off as he did when Fey called him a nursemaid. Trying to stay out of it—he as much as told Fey he could walk all over him.

Dane had said Fey and Tincher didn't have it in them to come at him face-to-face. Maybe they didn't, but they had it in them to do worse. Not having to look at someone's face would make it easier for them.

And he, Tom Atkins—what did he have in him? He knew no one would ask, but now on his own, he knew he had to face the question himself. Sure, if he had a chance he would fight for his life, but even the most lily-livered wretch would do that. What did he really have in him?

He recalled what Laurel had said about getting a gun and going after them herself. In some way, she meant it. Not only did she mean that she would do what she could, but she also meant she thought it would be justified if someone took an eye for an eye.

Atkins laughed. An eye for an eye and a tooth for a tooth. A fellow might feel shortchanged if all he got was Tincher.

When the laugh was over, Atkins got back on track with his thinking. Maybe he did have something in him—something more than the brave talk he had thrown out at Chapman, something more than Fey or Tincher would ever give him credit for. They thought he was as easy as an old whore, but that wouldn't keep them from trying. It might make them a little too confident, though. That was a good thought.

Atkins had another image of Laurel, alone in her own sense of futility. She probably hadn't given him any thought when she made that comment. It wouldn't have occurred to her to disapprove of him. She was just saying what she had in her. Well, maybe he had something in him, too. If there was one person left who could appreciate it, even as she said to hell with everything, it might be Laurel.

Atkins went to the sleeping room and took his rifle off the wall. Sitting once again in the chair, he held the rifle in his lap with his right hand on the stock. With his left, he ran the back of two fingers along the cold steel barrel. He had something in him. He didn't know how much, and he didn't have a plan. But he had something.

Chapter Fourteen

Atkins ran the back of his fingers along the cold steel barrel of the rifle once again. He told himself he had to be calm and careful. Maybe he was imagining danger, but he still needed to act with caution. Thinking back again on the conversation with Chapman, he recalled the storekeeper asking him if he would be out at the ranch alone. He doubted that it was a deliberate question, but he had given Chapman the information all the same. He shook his head. Fey would have an easy way of knowing when he was by himself without having to go to town to ask.

He looked at the woodbox and decided he should go fetch more firewood before he tended to the horses. Setting the rifle in the corner by the kitchen door, he glanced at the cookstove.

He could have beef and spuds for supper again, he imagined. The stove had probably gone all the way cold since the morning, but it wouldn't take him long to build up a fire and fry some grub. He stepped over to the stove, hefted the iron skillet with his right hand, and set it farther back on the stove as he held his left hand over the surface. No heat came through, just as he thought.

He put on his hat, coat, and gloves and went out into the winter afternoon. It was cold but not windy. Atkins looked around the ranch yard and, seeing nothing out of order, walked across to the woodpile. When he got there, he frowned. He thought he had more stove lengths already cut up. Diego must have brought in an armload or two while he was waiting. Well, that meant he was going to have to cut some more. It was a good thing he hadn't waited until the last minute.

With the ax in mind, he went to the door of the toolshed. As he reached to take the twig out of the hasp, he froze. The twig had been put in backwards. As a prickly feeling went through his neck and shoulders, Atkins made himself stop and think. He had gone into the toolshed a couple of times since Dane had gone on his last ride. As a matter of habit, he always put the twig in so that it looked like a Y, with the tail slanting down to the left. He had been doing it that way with the same twig for as long as he had been at the NB. It was one of the little things he did, out of his own sense of neatness, and he didn't recall ever mentioning it to anybody. He knew he hadn't put the twig in the hasp the other way, and seeing it rang a bell of caution. Someone else had put the twig there, and he doubted it had been Diego. If Diego had gone into the toolshed, he would have gone for the ax, and there would be more firewood cut. Atkins nodded. Someone else had gone into the toolshed. Someone else had been here.

Atkins glanced to his right. Whoever it was might be in the little house, but he doubted it. Still, rather than tip his hand and go back to the bunkhouse for the rifle, he decided to go to the stable and peek into the toolroom from there. Without looking again at the house, he went to the stable door, opened it, and left it that way to let in the daylight. Moving to the door that led to the toolroom, he lifted the latch. He heard nothing from within, so he opened the door a crack. He could see very little in the murky darkness, so he opened the door wider to let in some of the daylight that came in through the stable door. What he saw chilled his blood.

The dark, glistening barrel of a shotgun pointed at the door he had thought better of opening. He had heard of this sort of booby trap, but this was the first one he had ever seen. The stock of the shotgun was clamped in the vise that always sat in the toolroom, bolted to an old upright stump. As his vision adjusted to the dark interior, Atkins saw that a string ran from the trigger of the gun to a pulley on the back wall, then to a pulley on the rafter, and then to the door. Slack hung in the string—enough, Atkins figured, for a person to open the door all the way and then catch the full blast. It would also be enough slack for a person to edge out of the door after setting the trap. Whoever it was, he probably didn't know about the other door.

It had to be either Fey or Tincher, if not both. As Atkins thought back on it, he was quite sure Tincher had left the NB before this door got fixed. Yes, Tincher had left in the middle of the season, and Hal and Laurel brought back the hinges not long after that. If Tincher didn't know about the other door, then Fey didn't, and if anyone was watching, he wouldn't know what the man inside the stable was doing. Atkins nodded. And as far as that went, no one had to be watching. The engineer of this device could be off at a safe distance, waiting to hear the report of the shotgun.

Atkins shook his head and let out a long breath. All the time he had been sitting by the stove, thinking, and then holding the rifle in his lap, a loaded shotgun had been pointed at the door waiting for him. Someone had seen him leave with Diego and had taken the opportunity to slip in here and set things up.

Atkins stood for a moment with his hand on the open door, thinking of a plan. Whoever had set this trap didn't want to show himself. He would rather be a sneak, and he no doubt thought he was pretty clever. Maybe he was, but Atkins thought it might work the other way. He could try using the trap as a bait.

Leaving the door open, he stepped into the dark toolroom. He thought he should cut the string first, but then he decided against it. A little pressure in the wrong way could set off the gun and spoil everything, not to mention unnerve him. The first thing to do was unload the gun. It was a single-shot break-down model, so he pushed the lever with his right thumb and cupped his left hand over the breech to catch the shell. He had to shake the gun for the barrel to swing down, but it did, and the shell popped into his hand. After he had the gun unloaded, he cut the string. Then he looked around for just the right thing to have in hand in case he needed it. He picked up the crowbar and hefted it, then decided on the mattock. He could handle it better with both hands, and it had a good heavy end.

The plan was coming to him now. In a little while, just before dusk, he would open the door, load the shotgun, and set it off. He thought about loading the gun first, but he didn't like the idea of opening the door in front of the loaded weapon, even if he had cut the string. He thought also of going for the rifle, but it would be a tip-off if someone was watching. He knew he needed to leave the shotgun in place, so that the man who came a-sniffing would not see anything out of order in the first few seconds. If he had two or more shells, he could imagine using the first one to attract someone's attention and a second one to give him a surprise; but with just one shell, he decided to leave the shotgun in the vise. He would use the one shell to bring the other person out into the open.

He thought again of going for the rifle, but he found it distasteful to imagine cutting down a person in midstride. And if he tried to hold the other man at gunpoint, too many things could go wrong this far from town and anyone else. He would try to stun the other person, and then he could take it from there. He had to make his stroke a good one.

That was the way he would do it, he thought. He would hope he had only one man to contend with, and he would hope the other man's confidence would give him an edge. He realized he had been assuming this was the work of only one person, for it took only one to set up a job like that and wait somewhere in the cold shadows. If two men came, he was in trouble, but if there were two men out there waiting, he was in trouble no matter what.

Atkins felt himself getting cold. After the first

flush of excitement he had cooled down, and now his hands felt cold. He thought he could warm up by doing the chores, but he decided it would be better to stay out of sight. He stepped back out into the stable, where the light was a little better, and began stretching his arms back and forth across his chest to get the blood flowing. After fifty stretches he rested for a couple of minutes, then did fifty more. He was feeling calmer now, and warmer.

He looked out the stable doorway, but he couldn't see the sun because it set in the southwest during this time of the year. It was getting close to sundown, though—he knew that. The timing would help if he could manage it right. He swung his arms another fifty times, then decided to go outside for the one thing he had to do. Walking out and turning to the woodpile, he picked out one large, bare branch about six feet long. He lifted it, pivoted, and set it on his shoulder. Under cover of that maneuver he plucked the twig from the hasp, then walked back to the stable. He swung out to go through the doorway with the branch, and as he did so he caught a glimpse of the sun beyond the corner of the stable. It hung just above the mountains.

Setting the branch on the stable floor, he looked at the twig he held between the thumb and forefinger of his left gloved hand. It was just a little fork of dead wood, about four inches long and less than half an inch thick. He put it in his coat pocket, then took off his gloves and stuffed them in his pocket as well. Stepping back into the toolroom, he took a deep breath and reviewed his plan. Then he did it. In a moment he opened the door, loaded the shotgun, fired it, and took his place by the doorway with the mattock in hand. Then, as an afterthought, he tossed his hat on the floor where the weak daylight came in. That might hold someone's attention for a minute. Atkins held still now, with the mattock in both hands, the head of it above his right shoulder.

Standing in the shadow with the doorway on his left, he listened but heard nothing. The blast from the shotgun had filled the tool room for a second, but now there was only silence. The smell of gunpowder hung in the air, and he could see the muzzle of the shotgun. After several long minutes he thought he heard steps—soft steps, and from the sound of them, only one person. No voices, just soft steps coming closer.

Some of the daylight closed off in the doorway. Atkins heard someone breathing out through his nose. The man would be looking at the shotgun and the hat, wondering where the victim went. He might not have counted on having to look inside the dark room, so he would be hesitating.

The light, or blockage of it, moved. The person stepped up to the doorway, all a shadow, and then took a step forward—a person about the same height as Atkins, wearing a dark wool cap over his forehead and ears. When the man leaned forward toward the hat on the floor, Atkins swung.

He brought the mattock around and down with all his force, aiming the heavy iron shank at the back of the wool cap. The mattock connected with a solid thud, like the feeling Atkins knew from stunning an animal. The blow drove the man to the ground, and a six-gun spilled onto the floor in front of him. Atkins stood poised with the mattock, ready to swing again if he had to, but the man did not move. If he was not reaching for his gun, he must be out.

Atkins stepped around the man and thought of how he might pick up the gun. It was not cocked, but if he dragged it with the mattock he might set it off if it had a live round under the hammer. If he knelt, the man might come at him. He was pretty sure the man was out cold, but to make certain, he punched the head of the mattock at the man's right hand, which was bare and lay palm inward at his side. Getting no response, Atkins leaned down and picked up the six-gun. He unloaded all six shells, put them in his pocket, and set the pistol on the stump next to the vise. Then, remembering that another man might still be out there somewhere, he loaded five shells back into the cylinder and put the gun in his right coat pocket.

He had a pretty good idea of who the attacker was, but he rolled him over to get a better look. Weak light came straggling through the doorway, just enough for Atkins to verify the scruffy beard, the rough complexion, the lazy eye, and then the other eye, also dull, of Tincher.

Atkins let out a long breath. It came as no surprise that it was Tincher, but it still took a moment to absorb the full realization. The man had tried to kill him. Atkins wondered why Tincher had gone about it in this way, and he figured it was because Tincher would rather do something crafty, at a distance, than do it up close up and have to look Atkins in the face. So he had chosen to do it this way, as he had some familiarity with the layout of the NB and with the cook's habits. Well, it had fetched him a pretty good blow on the head, and he wouldn't feel so smart if he woke up in jail.

Atkins stepped over Tincher and pulled him aside so he wouldn't crush the hat any more. Atkins picked up the hat, punched it into shape, and brushed it off. As he put it on, he looked at Tincher's cap. Then he looked at the man's feet and saw he was wearing moccasins. That was another clever touch. A man could make less noise with them, and he would leave flatter footprints that would not match with his normal

261

ones. Atkins recalled Tincher's usual preference for big-heeled boots. Without the boots, he had looked shorter standing in the doorway.

The smile was gone from Tincher's face. If he thought he was clever, he was not smirking now. Atkins felt a little chill pass over him. He was so used to seeing Tincher's blank eye that it seemed normal for him to have his eyes open. At that thought, Atkins leaned over and felt the left wrist. Then he felt the neck. He looked at Tincher's face, rough and shadowy but blank. Tincher wasn't going to wake up, not in jail or anyplace else.

Atkins stood up and took another deep breath. He did not feel any remorse at discovering he had done in a man who had tried to do the same to him, but the outcome narrowed his thinking. Despite Tincher's protests, he and Fey had been in this conspiracy together. Fey had probably done the dirty work on both Hal and Dane, but Tincher was no innocent onlooker. He was in cahoots with Fey, and both of them were in the pay of Frank Cobarde, to rub out the Norden boys. Atkins was a material witness, and they had come after him. Tincher had failed, but there was no reason to think Fey wouldn't try.

Atkins looked down at the body on the floor. If he thought he was in deep before, he sure had to think it now. The difference was that he had taken action. He didn't have to wait for someone

to come after him now. He would be better off
not to, or he would always be looking over his
shoulder.

He thought of Fey, oiling his six-gun in the
bunkhouse of the Argentine Ranch, wondering
when Tincher would be coming back. Fey would
come looking. He would want to make sure the
job got done.

Atkins recalled Fey and his lean, malevolent
look. The darting eyes, the confident smile that
showed his teeth. Fey, who had done in the Norden boys and would come after him. Fey of the
silver spurs. Fey the assassin.

Well, thought Atkins, he wasn't going to sit
around and wait. He knew what he ought to do,
and he had an idea of how to do it.

The sun had set and the moon was on the rise
when he found Tincher's horse, a dark one like
before, tied to a cedar tree about half a mile north
of the ranch. Atkins led the horse back to the
stable and tied him up, then lit a lantern and saddled a horse for himself.

Now came the hard part, getting the body
loaded onto the horse. By tying up one leg, he
got the horse to keep still, but the dead, loose
weight was hard to lift that high. Dragging
Tincher through the toolroom and into the stable
had called for some effort on its own, and now
Atkins was trying to marshal up more strength
to hoist the body. As he rested from his first at-

tempt, he recalled Tincher's remark about the
cook being careful not to hurt himself by lifting
a quarter of a beef. Well, he thought, he'd get
this one lifted one way or another, even if he had
to hang him from the rafters with a rope on one
horse while he walked the other one under him.
After another try, and then a rest, he summoned
up the determination and got the body slumped
over the saddle of the dark horse.

After tying down the load, Atkins went for the
shotgun. It was useless to him because he had no
shells for it. He slipped it into Tincher's scabbard
and put the dead man's pistol in the saddlebag.
Then he went to the bunkhouse for his own six-
gun, plus his rifle and a scabbard, which he
strapped onto his own saddle. He was tired now,
but he had worked off most of his nervousness.
Having done everything all right so far, he felt
capable, even though he did not feel at leisure to
go cook and eat a meal. It would be a long night,
he thought, with plenty of time to spare, but he
did not want to spend any more of it here. He
went to the bunkhouse, rounded up a few cold
biscuits and a handful of dried apples, and went
back to the horses. After a glance around the inside of the stable, he blew out the lantern and
led the horses into the cold night.

Morning broke gray and cold along the Antelope
Breaks, where Atkins had decided to set his bait.

It would be a good morning for hunting coyotes, if a fellow knew where there was a dead cow and could find a good spot to hide nearby. Atkins had chosen the breaks because they had a thousand little clefts and nooks that would tire the eye of anyone riding through.

Atkins dumped Tincher facedown on the trail, with the six-gun in his holster and the shotgun beneath his arm. Then he smacked the horse on the rump, and it took off on a trot toward the Argentine Ranch. Atkins had left his own horse a mile back, tied to a box elder tree in a blind draw. A light snow was starting to fall as he climbed his way up into the breaks and looked for a spot to nestle into.

If the snow stuck at all, it should help Fey backtrack the horse and find Tincher. Fey would be leaving the Argentine bunkhouse by now, on the lookout for the dark horse.

Atkins stayed awake for what seemed like the first hour, letting his gaze rove across the landscape one way and then another. Then, as the day got a little older, he began to get drowsy. He would doze off and then wake with a start, thinking he had heard a voice or seen a rider. Being startled would keep him awake for a while, until drowsiness would begin to creep back upon him. He shifted in his seat, stretched his legs as much as he could. With the cloud cover he could not tell where the sun was, and with his dozing off he did not have a clear sense of how much time had gone by.

He wished he had something to eat. The dried apples and cold biscuits were long gone, and he wished he had taken the trouble to fix more grub. It hadn't seemed so important then, not with the urgency of getting out onto the trail. Now, as the morning seemed to drag on, he was hungry and sleepy. At moments the sleepiness came upon him so heavy that he thought he could go to sleep and not care about what happened. Then he sobered himself with the knowledge that he had better stay awake if he hoped ever to cook and eat another beefsteak.

His eyelids felt heavy and swollen as he blinked at the country around him. He wondered what he would do if he had to sit here all day until dark. He thought of how nice it would be to go back to the bunkhouse, where there was food and a warm cot. He shook his head again, telling himself there was no use thinking of those things when he was halfway into the worst part of it all.

From where he sat, a hundred and fifty yards away, he could see snow beginning to gather on Tincher's cap and coat. That meant all the warmth had gone out of Tincher. It also meant that if Fey didn't get here pretty soon, he wouldn't have a trail to follow. Atkins moistened his lips, blinked, and squinted. *Come on,* he thought.

Atkins opened his eyes with a start, clearing his head as fast as he could. He had fallen asleep. Off to his left now, coming from the west, was a lone rider. It looked larger than Fey. What would he do, he thought, if it were someone else? He couldn't shoot, and he couldn't just sit and wait until someone found him.

But it was Fey. He could tell now, from the broad-brimmed, flat-crowned hat. It was Fey, but in a larger overcoat, brown instead of gray. Atkins had been expecting the gray coat, had told himself to focus on the very center of it. As he felt his heartbeat quicken, he told himself again to aim at the dead center. The larger the target, the easier it was to get off center. It was like a coyote with his fur ruffed out—he looked like an easier target than he was.

Fey rode onward, his horse taking steady strides. The hat was not moving from side to side, so it looked as if Fey was keeping his eye on the form ahead of him on the trail.

Fey stopped fifty yards from the body. Now he looked around him, his chin lifted and his breath showing on the air. Atkins put his gloved left hand over his own mouth, lest a cloud give him away.

Now Fey moved forward again on his dark horse, stopping a few yards from the body and pulling the rifle from his scabbard as he dismounted. He stood at a three-quarter profile to Atkins, who had his rifle sights fixed on the brown coat. The perfect instant came, when he knew his aim, his heartbeat, the whole rhythm of the moment was right to pull the trigger. And he went past it.

Atkins felt a letdown, and he began to shake. He took a breath and let it out. He was going to have to try again.

Fey turned his back on Atkins and looked around to the northeast. That was normal, Atkins thought. If there was any sunlight at all, even behind a cloud, a person would rather look away from it than at it.

Fey turned back around and looked at the breaks where Atkins crouched. As the other man's gaze swept by, Atkins reached for help. He remembered Hal, and Dane, and Laurel, and two little boys wrapped up in blankets. Now he lined up the sights on the center of the brown coat. Fey was not going anywhere; he was turning back to his left, about to face the deadly spot a second time. It all came together again for Atkins—the perfect second in time in which he and his grip on the rifle were in harmony with the target—and he squeezed the trigger.

Fey's hat flew away as the gun barrel lifted and the sound of the gunshot rippled away through the breaks. Thin-legged Fey in the brown coat lay flat on his back, a couple of yards back from where he had stood. His rifle lay on the ground at his feet, and his dark horse was galloping toward Silver Mountain.

Atkins moistened his lips. He was shaking now, but he made himself keep his calm. If he saw any motion at all, he was going to have to shoot again before he came out of his nest. If one shot had done it, he needed to get back to town as soon as he could.

The sun still hadn't come out. He had no idea what time it was, but he couldn't wait all day. After a few more minutes of seeing no movement, Atkins got up and walked down to the spot where the two bodies lay. Fey's mouth and eyes were open, and his teeth looked yellow in the white morning. Atkins watched as a large snowflake landed on Fey's right eye and turned to water. Another fell on his left cheekbone and melted. Atkins nodded and took off on a fast walk for his horse.

It was a ranch horse, a big sorrel that Dane had ridden. It covered the ground fast with a steady lope. Atkins slowed him to a walk a couple of times, but the sorrel seemed willing to keep at it, so Atkins let him out.

Snow was piling up when they came to town. That was good, Atkins thought. It made things quiet and it would cover tracks. Rather than ride down the main street, Atkins rode around to the

269

John D. Nesbitt

south side and came in on a back street. He put
the horse in the stable behind Ralph and Susie's
house and went on in through the back door.

Laurel met him with little Hal in her arms.
"My God, Tom, what's happened? Did you just
come from the ranch?"

"I came from out that way. What time is it,
anyway?"

"It's about half past ten."

"Whew. I would have thought it was later."

"You look worn out. What happened?"

"They came after me," he said.

"And you got away?"

He winced. "Not real easy. I had to club
Tincher, but I got it done. And then I put a bullet
through Fey."

"And where are they now? Are they on their
way here?"

Atkins shook his head. "Oh, no. They're both
lyin' on the trail out by the Antelope Breaks.
They're not goin' anywhere until someone finds
'em."

Laurel's blue-gray eyes had widened. "My
God, Tom. You mean you—?"

"I had to. I really didn't have any choice. They
came after me."

Laurel had a triumphant look on her face.
"And you got them both?"

Atkins swallowed. "Uh-huh. I don't know

270

what I'll say if someone comes questioning me, but that's the way it happened."

"Tom," she said, smiling as she shook her head. "You couldn't have done any such a thing."

Atkins let out a short, heavy sigh. "The hell I couldn't! It halfway killed me, just the toll it took on my nerves. Maybe they didn't think I could, but I sure as hell did."

"No, Tom," she said, shaking her head. "You couldn't have done such a thing." She smiled. "I'll tell anyone who pries it out of me. You spent the whole night here with me."

Chapter Fifteen

Atkins hung his coat on the iron hook in the entryway, then set his hat on the protruding point of the coat. As he walked into the living room, Laurel appeared at the doorway that led to the kitchen. The gaslight in the front room cast a faint shine on the gray hair that showed at her temples.

"I thought it was you," she said.

"Are the boys home?"

"No, they went back out to run around with their friends."

Atkins looked at her and nodded. She did not look as tired today as she sometimes did. Her blue-gray eyes had a light in them, and her dark hair made a sharp contrast with the light complexion of her face. Life showed in her features.

She was always a pretty woman, but she showed it more on some days, like today.

"Well," he said, "I heard they sure-enough hanged Tom Horn."

Laurel gave a slight nod. "That's what the boys said. I think they wanted to go back out and talk about it with their friends."

"No harm in that, I suppose."

"No, not really. I told them to be sure to be back in time for supper."

Atkins looked around the room. "Well, I think I'll sit down for a while." He looked back at Laurel.

"Go ahead." She smiled. "You look like you had a long day. It won't be long till supper." She turned and went back into the kitchen.

Atkins watched her until she moved out of sight. She had filled out a little in the last few years, but she was still pretty—more than he deserved, he thought, but he wouldn't quibble.

He took the iron poker from its stand and shaped up the burning logs in the fireplace. He set the poker back in its place, put on two more pieces of firewood, and pulled the wooden armchair close to the fire.

He let out a long breath as he sat down. The hanging of Tom Horn gave him plenty to think about. The event meant different things to different people, from those who thought he should go free to those who thought he should have gotten it a long time ago. For Atkins, it came down to the well-known truth that Horn was a hired killer. Maybe he wasn't so low as to kill the kid up by Iron Mountain, and maybe the person who did—Horn or someone else—thought he was aiming at the kid's father. That didn't matter to Atkins. This fellow Horn had gotten away with killing men until it suited someone's purposes to get him convicted and finally hanged. Whether he had killed the kid or not, and whether he was being punished for his crimes or for someone's political benefit, the outcome was that a paid killer got stretched. Atkins could not complain, and he didn't think Laurel would, either. At the same time, though, he knew that one event didn't fix anything.

Atkins counted back the years. It had been more than twelve, almost thirteen, years since that winter morning out by the Antelope Breaks. It had been a lot for him to do at the time, but he hadn't done that much. He had stopped Fey and Tincher, nothing more, and they had already done more than anyone could make up for. And no one seemed to care—not about Hal's death, or Dane's, or the death of Cobarde's two hired men. Life went on. Cobarde seemed to pull in his horns after that, but if he had been better connected to some of the other big cattlemen, he might not have. Laurel sold the NB to a new outfit that eventually took over the Argentine Ranch as well, so that Cobarde, after all his ambitions, went somewhere else. Atkins had never heard of him after he left Wyoming.

As for the other big cattlemen, they went right along with their own methods. When the Sweetwater ranchers got away with the Cattle Kate lynching, others seemed to have grown bolder. Not long after the Norden trouble, a man named Tisdale had been killed up in the Powder River country, and in the following spring, a whole army of men, most of them hired guns from Texas, had killed Nate Champion and Nick Ray up in the same area. The big augurs did what they wanted and eventually got away with it. Sure, there had been investigations and inquests, but no punishments, and even after that, they continued to bring in fellows like Tom Horn.

Atkins nodded as he gazed at the fire. He had been lucky to be able to do what he did and get out. If Cobarde had made better alliances, or if someone had cared more about Fey and Tincher, then at some time or another, Atkins might have heard a voice over his shoulder.

But he hadn't, and he doubted that he would. Laurel's alibi had been enough at the time, and then they had moved to Laramie. He was sure that people around Farris, not to mention Ralph and Susie, thought he was an opportunist, exploiting the vulnerable girl who had to sell her ranch. That was all right, if it gave him cover and it didn't travel far or last long. Here in Laramie, he was just another working man, a common boardinghouse cook who was helping his wife raise her two sons.

As for the boys, known around town as the Norden boys, they didn't seem to care all that much about him, either. They idolized their fathers and wanted to be cowboys with their own ranch. Atkins didn't know about that. They'd have to make it on their own, like their fathers did. Laurel's money had been stretched thin, and he didn't have anything to help them get started. They knew that. He could tell they looked at him as someone who didn't make enough money and who didn't deserve their mother. But they were young, Dane having turned fourteen and Hal about to turn thirteen. They were just learning how to raise hell, so it would be a long time, if ever, until they appreciated the old man who sat by the fire, the one they would never call Dad.

Not that he was that old. He still had a full head of hair, even if most of it was gray. He could still work, and that mattered. He could still ride when he had to, and his hands had not forgotten the feel of a rope. Maybe his wife was younger and would have enjoyed someone closer in age, but the two of them were raising the boys, and that counted the most. Laurel had known true love once, it had been taken away, and she didn't seem to expect to find it again. For his part, Atkins loved her and knew she loved him in her own way, but he knew it wasn't the same as she had known with Hal. That was all right, too.

Laurel appreciated him, and that went a long ways. Maybe someday, after he was gone, she would be able to tell the boys that he wasn't such a bad sort and that at one moment, at least, he had what it took. In the meanwhile, given the circumstances, it was enough that Laurel knew. They had patched together a family and were doing all right. On a day like today, when he remembered the pain of the old stuff, he found satisfaction in knowing she appreciated what he had done for the Norden boys.

Man From Wolf River

John D. Nesbitt

Owen Felver is just passing through. He is on his way from the Wolf River down to the Laramie Mountains for some summer wages. He makes his camp outside of Cameron, Wyoming, and rides in for a quick beer. But it isn't quick enough. While he is there he sees pretty, young Jenny—and the puffed-up gent trying to get rude with her. What else can he do but step in and defend her? Right after that some pretty tough thugs start to make it clear Felver isn't all too welcome around town. Trouble is, the more they tell him to move on—and the more he sees of Jenny—the more he wants to stay. He knows they have something to hide, but he has no idea just how awful it is—or how far they will go to keep it hidden.

___4871-X $4.50 US/$5.50 CAN

Coyote Trail

John D. Nesbitt

Travis Quinn doesn't have much luck picking his friends. He is fired from the last ranch he works on when a friend of his gets blacklisted for going behind the owner's back. Guilt by association sends Quinn looking for another job, too. He makes his way down the Powder River country until he runs into Miles Newman, who puts in a good word for him and gets him a job at the Lockhart Ranch. But Quinn doesn't know too much about Newman, and the more he learns, the less he likes. Pretty soon it starts to look like Quinn has picked the wrong friend again. And if the rumors about Newman are true, this friend might just get him killed.

____4671-7 $4.50 US/$5.50 CAN

WILD ROSE of RUBY CANYON

JOHN D. NESBITT

At first homesteader Henry Sommers is pleased when his neighbor Van O'Leary starts dropping by. After all, friends come in handy out on the Wyoming plains. But it soon becomes clear that O'Leary has some sort of money-making scheme in the works and doesn't much care how the money is made. Henry wants no part of his neighbor's dirty business, but freeing himself of O'Leary is almost as difficult as climbing out of quicksand . . . and just as dangerous.

___4520-6 $3.99 US/$4.99 CAN

Dorchester Publishing Co., Inc.
P.O. Box 6640
Wayne, PA 19087-8640

Please add $1.75 for shipping and handling for the first book and $.50 for each book thereafter. NY, NYC, and PA residents, please add appropriate sales tax. No cash, stamps, or C.O.D.s. All orders shipped within 6 weeks via postal service book rate. Canadian orders require $2.00 extra postage and must be paid in U.S. dollars through a U.S. banking facility.

Name_____
Address_____
City_____State_____Zip_____
I have enclosed $_____ in payment for the checked book(s).
Payment <u>must</u> accompany all orders. ❑ Please send a free catalog.
CHECK OUT OUR WEBSITE! www.dorchesterpub.com

Jane Candia Coleman

THE O'KEEFE EMPIRE

Alex O'Keefe has a dream. Fired up with visions of an empire and millions of acres for the taking in New Mexico Territory, he sets out from Texas to make his dream a reality. His wife, Joanna, becomes caught up in her husband's enthusiasm, sells the family holdings, then boards a train to meet him. She has no idea what lies before her. When Joanna arrives, her own dreams are nearly shattered. Alex is dead, murdered by an unknown killer. And the empire they had planned is threatened by exorbitant cattle fees charged by the railroad. But dreams die hard. Joanna will do whatever she has to, even if that means taking the cattle on a brutal overland trail drive to San Diego, across the Mojave Desert.

___4859-0 $4.50 US/$5.50 CAN